The Portal
&
The Experiment

Two Novellas of Suspense

Also by Lynn L. Clark

The Home Child
Fire Whisperer & Circle of Souls
The Accusers

The Portal
&
The Experiment

Two Novellas of Suspense

Lynn L. Clark

The Plaid Raccoon Press

2018

Book design & cover design by Michael J. McCann
Front Cover photographs: mg7 & pashabo/ Thinkstock
Back cover photograph: MorelSO/Thinkstock

www.theplaidraccoonpress.com

THE PORTAL

For my mother-in-law,
Janet Irene McCann,
in memory of
gentler times.

1

My name is Emily Montfort. When I was young, I thought my last name sounded quite exotic and that my ancestors were probably castle dwellers of noble descent. I was very creative in building my own mythology.

Nowadays I don't have the time or inclination for fantasies. I'm a pragmatic thirty-four year old living in Ottawa, Ontario, Canada's capital city.

I'm an only child. My mother developed Alzheimer's disease about three years before her death, and I became her caregiver. For those who've never witnessed the disease's ravaging effects on the mind and then, gradually, the body, I can only envy you and say that I truly hope you don't have to undergo this tragedy with someone you love. By the time my mother died, she'd gone from the slightly mischievous, quick-witted woman I'd known all my life to someone I didn't even recognize.

My mother was predeceased by my father so when she died, I inherited their small antique shop.

I live in an apartment above the shop. I have only to descend and mount the stairs—day and evening—to get to and leave work.

It's very convenient, if a bit circumscribing.

2

My parents were never major players in the competitive Ottawa antique business, but they were well-known for their contributions to the community. In addition to purchasing antiques, they bought beds, mattresses, couches, dishes, and other serviceable items they would donate to local homeless shelters and charities. Whenever there was news of a family displaced by a fire, I remember my mom being on the phone to the Salvation Army asking how she could help. So I was not surprised that my mother's funeral—and my father's before her—was so well-attended. Mom, no doubt, would have taken it in stride, but would have been secretly pleased at the turnout.

I remember one day at the beginning of her illness, I'd been reading to her until she fell asleep. I'd placed the book on my lap and was staring off into space, feeling particularly miserable, when suddenly I realized she was awake and watching me with her beautiful cornflower blue eyes. It was one of her rare moments of lucidity.

'Please don't be so sad, Em. I know what's happening to me, and I'm grieving inside, and part of me is mad as hell and saying this can't be happening. But it's going to be harder for you than me, Em. And I want you to know something. And I'll say it now before I forget. I'm an ordinary person who's lived an ordinary life. I've known sorrows and I've known happiness, and I did the best I could with what I was given. I loved your father even though I could have cheerfully strangled him at times for his obstinacy. And I love you with all my heart and I'm so proud of you.

"Listen to me," she laughed, "your father would say I'm waxing philosophical again. Such a die-hard stoic he was." Her eyes misted with the memory of him.

"This isn't coming out the way I wanted it to, it's so difficult for me to concentrate any more, but while I still have a few thoughts to cobble together, I just want to tell you that it's okay to grieve for me after my death. But for my sake and yours, promise me you'll move on with your life."

Mom gradually lost even the power of speech as the disease advanced. This would be the last time she spoke coherently to me.

3

hen I was a teenager I used to love the weekend junkets I made with my parents in search of antiques. My parents had a standing wish list from their steady customers of items to look for on these trips. Sometimes we'd free-style in the small towns and countryside outside Ottawa. On these occasions we'd pack a picnic lunch and take in both advertised and unadvertised yard sales, checking for smaller items: primarily brass belt buckles, coins, and pocket watches. Occasionally we'd come across a real treasure such as an antique washstand barely recognizable beneath its layers of paint or a solid brass spittoon.

Of course my parents relied extensively on auctions and estate sales to replenish their stock. I was allowed to attend these events from a very early age with the understanding that I wouldn't try to bid on anything. For the most part, these gatherings in the countryside had a convivial and informal atmosphere that did not prevail at the stricter and more expensive auctions conducted in Ottawa where it was a given that items would fetch higher prices.

My father had grown up in Fredericton, New Brunswick, and had come to the nation's capital to study engineering at Carleton University. My mother, on the other hand, hailed from a small town in the Ottawa Valley. While my father had a dry—some would say non-existent—sense of humour, my mother loved to laugh and play jokes on people. How the two of them ever got together I'm not really sure, although I know they adored each other. My dad died of a heart attack shortly after their fortieth anniversary. Mom outlived him by almost a decade.

Dad was always looking for highway signs during these trips and cursing because there were so few of them. My mother would laugh at him and say, "We're out in the country now, dear, and the people who live here know there are only limited ways to get from one place to another. *They* obviously don't need signs to tell them that."

4

It's been almost three months since my mother died, and the stock in the store is getting low so I've decided to embark on my first solo trip to make the circuit of yard sales, auctions, and estate sales. I know these journeys will never be quite the same without both of my parents: already I miss Mom's incessant chatter. But it's a beautiful early spring day, and I'm taking the back roads and am proud of myself that I recognize so many of the landmarks.

I drive past small churches with handwritten signs advertising their next services; local Masonic and legion halls with their announcements of bingo and upcoming fish fries; and the returning Canada geese walking in the spring run-off in fields by the roadside. These are my mom's people who populate this countryside: the ones who always infuriated her with their small- and capital-C conservatism, but whom she steadfastly supported because of their hard work and fierce loyalty to family and friends.

My first stop is at Dorothy Miller's house. She's a long-time family friend who's been selling antiques to us since I was a small child. Dorothy sent me a sympathy card after my mom's death, apologizing for not attending the funeral and explaining that she doesn't drive any more because of her rheumatoid arthritis.

I travel up the long gravel driveway that leads to her house, and Dorothy is at the door to greet me before I'm even out of the car. I haven't seen her for several years and so, as she opens the sagging wooden screen door to hug me, it's a shock to see how much she's aged. Her fingers are swollen and gnarled on the wooden cane supporting her, and she walks with a swaying limp.

She tells me again how sorry she is not to have been at my mother's funeral and how fond she was of both my parents. I have to keep reminding myself even now that no one person has a monopoly on grief: each of the people who came to the funeral home or to the store in the months after my mother's death had his or her own story to share—as Dorothy does—of how they would miss her, how she had touched their lives.

By tacit consent, Dorothy and I do not discuss how my mother died. It's as if Alzheimer's disease is the new cancer for many of the elderly, and they superstitiously refuse to talk about it as if they can somehow avoid bringing this misfortune upon themselves.

When we're seated on the shabby couch in the living room, Dorothy offers me lemonade. I start to refuse because I hate to see her struggling with her limited mobility, but then I realize she's probably been preparing all morning for my visit and will be deeply disappointed if I decline the refreshments. As a compromise I suggest that we move to the kitchen table to be more comfortable, and then I'm able to help her serve the lemonade and the batch of chocolate chip cookies she's baked herself.

"So, Emmie" (she is one of the few people who calls me this), "I phoned you last week because I've finally decided to get rid of John's box camera collection and that magic lantern and slides your parents always admired."

She makes it sound as if they're just taking up too much space, but I know that she would only part with her husband's collection because she needs the money. I expect the small pension cheques she receives barely cover her lights and heat.

We move once again into the living room where she has the box cameras—one hundred or so—proudly displayed on shelves on an end wall. For a moment I feel such an overwhelming sadness and anger at her poverty that I clench my fists and I don't trust myself to speak. Thankfully, Dorothy has not noticed. She wouldn't want me to feel sorry for her.

"My husband brought some of these back from Europe after the war. He was in Normandy, but I think I've probably told you that before. Anyway, the magic lantern and slides were a childhood gift from his parents." She points to the early projector that is massive, but intricate in its design, almost a work of art.

I'm not an expert in box cameras, but I know that some of these models are fairly common while others are more valuable. In the end, I overpay Dorothy for the lot. I think she knows that I've done this, but doesn't say anything because she assumes that I'm struggling with the business since my mother's death and doesn't want to hurt my feelings. Instead, she quietly adds a metal bed warming pan, a lovely crumb duster tray set, and some old ice tongs to the box, as well as giving me a huge plastic freezer bag with the rest of the cookies.

It's been a complicated dance between the two of us as it often is in the countryside where poverty and dignity collide, but we get through it okay, and I hug her good-bye and promise to visit again soon.

As I'm driving away, I realize that it's almost noon, and I'm starving in spite of the cookies. I remember there's a restaurant nearby in a lovely old converted stone house. It's pricey, I know, but I'm assuming the lunch menu is more reasonable.

5

approach the restaurant and see Lexuses and BMWs parked haphazardly like getaway cars on the far side of the road. I've heard the restaurant is a favourite stop for rich Americans. I park in the small parking lot beside the restaurant. It's almost empty, perhaps because the rich folks are afraid of having their cars side-swiped in such a small space. I enter and the owner shows me to a table and hands me a menu.

I've only been here once before, but I remember the displays of antiques and Royal Family memorabilia. My eyes scan the shelves as I wait for my meal. There are some lovely old dishes as well as military photos of soldiers long-lost to war.

The building is supposed to be haunted because of a death that occurred when it was still a family home. The story goes that one day the staff saw a teapot fly across the room and crash against a wall. The dented teapot is now proudly on display in the restaurant. I'm sure this story adds to the mystique of the place, but I don't give much credence to ghosts.

****

I'm back on the road now, and as I pass an old farmhouse, I see there's a crowd gathered out front. Curious, I pull into the driveway and discover there's an estate sale in progress. I park the car and look around at the items displayed on the lawns. Men are examining tractors and farm equipment, while the women slowly stroll the tables of antique lacework and dishes. A friendly Border Collie runs over to me, and I pat his head until he gets bored and wanders off again.

It seems to be mostly local people here, although I recognize a few dealers who have already staked out the most valuable antiques. As I navigate the furniture, I come upon an old tiger stripe dresser that stands out like a brave orphan in a sea of headboards and mattresses. Its mirror is starting to de-silver, and there is a large water stain on top of the dresser that greatly decreases its value, but it's a beautiful piece, and no one seems particularly interested in it.

I register in the house and get my number, and then sit to one side on an old wooden bench while I wait patiently for the auctioneer to get to the furniture section. He's wiping his face with his ball cap, and I can see that he's tired and wants to wrap up the auction before his voice gives out. He's probably been at this since early morning.

When he comes to the dresser, I find that I'm excited. I'd really like to have this piece in spite of its imperfections. The bidding is desultory, and he's about to declare the item sold when I hold up my number and bid a higher price. No one challenges me. The dresser is mine.

I also buy the leftover mattresses, bed frames, and headboards, as well as some household appliances and dishes. I plan to continue my parents' practice of donating durable goods to local shelters and charities. I am keenly aware that Ottawa is a city of haves and have-nots. There are the mansions of Rockcliffe, the diplomats in their ostentatious cars, the sprawl of the

U.S. Embassy, and the flux of government workers. But there are also the damaged, homeless people who are largely invisible in the city.

****

My family has always relied upon a Kemptville man with a small moving and cleanup company to deliver large purchases to our store in Ottawa. I have one of his crumpled business cards in my purse, and so I call him now from my cellphone. He's glad to hear from me: perhaps he's been uncertain whether I planned to continue giving him business. He agrees to meet me here with his truck.

I shake his hand when he arrives, and he tells me he's had heart surgery and can no longer lift.

"I use the young'uns for that." He grins, and then points his cane at the dresser and other items I've purchased and issues instructions to his helpers.

I thank him and decide to call it a day. It's getting late and besides I've closed the shop to come down here.

6

It's Sunday, and I'm waiting for Ed Scott to deliver my purchases from yesterday's estate sale.

I've accepted the fact that I can't keep the shop going by myself, and have placed an ad in the local paper to find someone who can relieve me in the store when I'm on buying trips or just need a day off. I'll be starting the interviews on Monday. I'm in my office at the shop right now, going over the resumes I've received. I realize I'm looking for a clone of my mother: someone good-natured, but practical-minded, efficient, and knowledgeable of antiques and the current market. I know this is just a pipe dream. I will never be able to replace her.

I hear the knock at the back door and go to let Ed Scott and his helpers in. There's a backroom that serves as storage for extra stock and furniture that needs repair or refinishing. Ed's helpers bring the dresser and other items into the room, and after I've paid him and we've said our good-byes, I look once again at the dresser, wondering vaguely why I'm so attracted to it. I try to pull out the top drawer because frequently there are newspapers used as linings in these old dressers that help to date them. But the drawer sticks because the wood has warped with age, and I leave it, not wanting to cause damage. I'll bring some paraffin wax out later to treat it.

I finger the water stain on top of the dresser. It looks worse than I remember. I don't plan to strip the varnish because it will harm the tiger stripe. It's called that because the wood—usually oak—has distinctive dark, wavy lines that resemble tiger stripes. I'll need to do some research to see if there's any way to remove the water stain without damaging the wood. My mother was always good at things like this. I'll need to teach myself more about furniture restoration.

As I move away from the dresser, I happen to glance in the mirror. In addition to my own reflection, I see a flash of ill-fitting dark clothing, and for a moment I could swear that a gentleman, dressed in a suit that must have dated to the nineteenth century, is staring absently out at me.

****

Although I've tried to busy myself in the shop, my hands are still shaking from the incident in the backroom a few hours ago. I'm wondering if it was the old photographs in the restaurant yesterday that made me imagine I saw someone in the mirror.

I square my shoulders and shake my head to dispel the image. But I'm still deeply troubled because it seemed so real to me.

7

It's Monday morning, and I have four interviews scheduled for the part-time job. My 9 AM appointment is running late: not a good sign. The bell over the door finally rings, and a short female with enormous blue eyes and wild curly blond hair walks into the store.

"Can I help you, miss?"

"Hi, I'm Carrie Morrison. Here for the job interview." She thrusts out her hand for me to shake. "Sorry I'm late. Blasted OC Transpo changed its schedule again. You have to be a mind-reader to know when to catch a bus in this city."

As I shake her hand, I realize that I'm

staring at her, but I can't seem to help it. She looks all of twelve.

Seeing my expression, she laughs. "You know I often leave people at a loss for words."

Recovering myself, I lead her to my corner desk and offer her a chair. As the interview proceeds, I realize with slight amazement that she is not only highly articulate, but well-schooled in antiques primarily because, she explains, her parents are avid collectors.

"I have a totally useless degree in Art History," she tells me, "that I knew would be useless even before I started university, but which I was obstinate—okay, perverse—enough to pursue. I'm working to save up for my own studio some day." She looks a little embarrassed by this admission.

"Luckily for me, as far as this job goes, I grew up in a family of collectors—hoarders is such an unkind word, don't you think?—and I developed a love for antiques from an early age." She winks at me. "It was a matter of survival: my parents probably would've disowned me otherwise."

When the interview ends, she lightly fingers the desk where we've been seated and says, "This is a lovely old piece. You don't see workmanship like this any more," she points to the ornate inlay, "and the mahogany is beautifully oiled. I see the chairs match as well. Late nineteenth century I would guess based on the cut iron nails that are burred on one side."

And then she adds, "Oh, by the way, did I mention that I'm very happy to work evenings and weekends?"

In truth, I find her to be quite charming, and I especially admire her youth and energy.

8

Carrie's been working in the shop for about a month now and has been a great help to me. She's won over my customers—even the stiff Rockcliffe matrons—with her enthusiasm and knowledge of antiques.

Sometimes I think she's my alter ego. We're not only opposites in terms of appearance—I'm tall and pale with dark hair that I wear in a bun—and she's barely five feet tall with her beautiful corona of blond curls and her complexion shining with the ruddy glow of youth. While I tend to be introspective and quiet, Carrie talks in an intimate and almost conspiratorial tone that automatically puts you at ease and makes you want to smile—something I don't do very often any more.

I'm in the backroom now, while Carrie's looking after the shop.

I'm ashamed to admit that I've hung a sheet over the dresser mirror since that day when I thought I saw someone in it. Today I've managed to dislodge the drawer that was sticking. As I suspected, there are some yellowing newspapers inside. I'm going through them now. They are old copies of the *Daily Telegraph and Courier*, as it was then called, from Britain. The edges are worn, and I can just barely see a date of 1860, which would place the newspapers in the Victorian Age.

Part of me loves that era because of its literature and art. The other part recognizes the hypocrisy of the Victorian Age: the wealthy covering the legs of pianos to avoid the appearance of indecency while giving little thought to the poor children, who toiled endlessly in the factories or roamed the streets because they were homeless.

I'm lost in thought for a few moments, but when I glance up suddenly, I see that the sheet has been dislodged from the mirror, probably as a result of my pulling on the drawer.

I stare into the pleading eyes of a gaunt man in an ill-fitting black suit.

This time I don't recoil from the sight.

I ask him simply: "What do you want of me?"

9

I've been at my desk most of the morning, reading through the old newspapers I found yesterday while Carrie waits on the customers. I've seen her glance my way several times, and she's offered to make me a cup of tea, which I politely declined.

"Where'd you find those?" I realize she's standing over me. I know she's asked me a question, but I was lost in thought and didn't hear her.

"I'm sorry, what did you say?"

"I was just wondering where the newspapers came from."

"Oh. I found them in the drawer of the tiger stripe dresser back there. I'm trying to see if I can get any idea of its provenance."

"I love that dresser, but it has a serious

water stain. Do you want me to try to remove it? I'll be very careful not to damage the wood."

"No, Carrie," I say, almost wildly, "please leave it alone. I'll take care of it, I promise."

She looks at me strangely, but says nothing.

****

I'm surprisingly calm in spite of the second appearance of the man in the mirror. I've spent the rest of the day going through the various newspapers, trying to find some clue to his identity. In fact, I can't believe I'm being this calm.

I've scoured the obituaries in the newspapers, and I can't find anything that connects to the man in the mirror. I've also made a list of genealogical websites I can consult, but at this point it's like finding a needle in a haystack.

10

It's been two weeks since I last glimpsed the man in the mirror. He hasn't appeared to me since.

As I expected, the search of websites has been useless. I don't have a date of birth or death. I don't have a name.

I'm going back this evening after Carrie leaves.

****

Carrie just went to catch her bus. She has a small apartment in the west end of Ottawa: too far away for her to walk to the shop. She's explained her ongoing problem catching the buses on time because of route changes and constant traffic delays in a city that is always under construction. I've told her not to worry about it and have given

Carrie her own key to the store as a sign of my trust in her.

I lock the door of the shop and enter the backroom. The sheet no longer covers the mirror even though I know I replaced it the last time I was here.

I pull over a chair and sit in front of the dresser. It takes me several moments to gather the courage to look into the mirror.

He is there again, my man in the mirror, as substantial as life although I know he must have died over a century ago.

The rational part of my brain tells me this is ridiculous, the result of an overwrought mind still grieving from my mother's death.

But the lizard part of my brain keeps telling me that he is real.

"Can you speak to me? Are you capable of communicating between our two worlds?"

By way of answer, he does not speak, but instead gestures to the dresser drawer, which I now notice is open. I reach in and extract a tintype photograph inserted in a cardboard backing. I look from the photo to the man in the mirror: they are one and the same.

In the Victorian age, young children and, less frequently, adults were photographed post mortem, with the pictures serving as mementoes for their loved ones. The mounted photos are often called "mourning cards" and are quite valuable nowadays. I've seen several of them, but I've never stocked them in my shop because they're so macabre. The idea of photographing the dead is repulsive to me.

I turn over the cardboard backing in which the photograph has been inserted and find the name "Edward" inscribed along with a date of 1860—presumably the year of his death.

Finally, I have some way of searching his identity, although the information is scant.

I look up into the mirror, but Edward is no longer there, and I feel an inexplicable sense of loss.

As I'm about to return to the shop, a blackness envelops the mirror, and I see a glint of metal.

An amorphous face springs from the darkness, its eyes glowing red and its mouth curved in a sneer.

I know instinctively this isn't Edward. I'm in the presence of someone— or something—inherently evil.

The face is suspended in the blackness for several minutes. The air in the room grows foul and suffocating, and I'm nauseous with a feeling of claustrophobia. A torpor has overtaken me, and I'm unable to move as I stare into the abyss of the mirror.

Finally, the blackness dissipates and the mirror clears. The face is gone.

I'm able to move again as if a spell has been lifted from me, and I run from the room, slamming and locking the door behind me.

11

I'm still unnerved by the ghastly face I saw in the mirror earlier this evening. I've moved a heavy steamer trunk against the door, although I know in my heart that this malignant force can not be stopped by such a paltry barrier. My hands are shaking violently as I search the newspapers from the dresser once again for some clue to Edward's identity.

I come across an article relating to a death by stabbing:

> A Good Samaritan who tried to intervene when a young woman was being assaulted Saturday evening was stabbed by the woman's attacker, who fled the scene of the attack. When police arrived, the gentleman

was already bleeding profusely. He died two hours later in hospital. The young woman also fled the scene. Police are currently conducting inquiries related to the identities of the three persons....

I start looking through the other newspapers and see a follow-up article:

The man who died in the knife attack known as the Good Samaritan murder has been identified as Edward Fitzmorris. Mr. Fitzmorris was 32 years old and unmarried. His body was identified by his brother, Patrick. The killer of Mr. Fitzmorris remains at large.

So I now know Edward's surname and the violent manner of his death.

Was the evil face I saw in the mirror that of his murderer and the metal I glimpsed momentarily the killer's knife?

12

I t's Sunday and I have the shop to myself. I didn't sleep well last night, thinking of the face in the mirror. I've decided to spend the day on my computer trying to piece together the history of Edward Fitzmorris.

I go first to a British genealogy site and type in his name and date of birth and death since I know he died when he was thirty-two years old. I learn that Edward died on September 9, 1860. I search the newspapers from the dresser, and spot the obituary I've previously passed over:

> Edward Osborne Fitzmorris was buried today after a commemoration of his life in a church service led by the Reverend James Holloway. Mr.

Fitzmorris died at the age of 32 at the hands of an unidentified assailant. He was pre-deceased by his father, Raymond Edward Fitzmorris, and his mother, Gail Catherine Fitzmorris, nee Osborne. He is survived by his brother, Patrick, and his sister, Edna.

I decide to search the names of Edward's siblings in the genealogy database. After several false starts—there are surprisingly many people with the same name—I'm able to find the date of his brother Patrick's death, but nothing for the sister.

Then a thought strikes me, and I do a Google search for the estate sale where I bought the dresser. I find a newspaper notice advertising the sale of the estate of the late Frank and Sarah Cunningham. When I search for their obituaries, I discover the link to Canada. In Sarah Cunningham's obituary, I learn that her mother's maiden name was Fitzmorris and that she immigrated to Canada in the late nineteenth century. This would explain how the dresser got to Canada: it was probably brought over as part of her mother's personal effects when she emigrated from Britain.

I'm not sure where to go from here. I

could try to contact one of Frank and Sarah's children, but what more could they tell me? I probably know more now about the provenance of the dresser than they do.

I rub my eyes and start to make myself a cup of tea when I hear a loud crash from the backroom. Startled but feeling braver in the light of day, I move aside the steamer trunk, unlock the door, and open it.

The tintype of Edward Fitzmorris lies on the floor along with a heavy pair of antique scissors.

The photograph has been cut into so many pieces that it is beyond repair.

But even more disturbing is the overwhelming presence of evil I once again sense in the room.

13

Another week has passed since the incident with the tintype. I haven't had the nerve to go back there again.

It's Saturday, and I've overslept and can already hear Carrie moving around in the shop below. It's unlike me to be so careless with the time, but lately I find that I'm experiencing bouts of insomnia: I lie awake for hours and then finally fall asleep about 5 AM.

I dress quickly and rush down the stairs into the shop. But as usual, Carrie has everything under control and has even found the time to make me a pot of tea. How is it that this young woman—twenty-two years old—can suddenly be such a stabilizing influence in my life?

I join Carrie at the desk and see that she's sorting through some pocket watches while alternately doing internet searches at my computer, which I've told her she is free to use. It's not yet 9 AM—our opening time on Saturdays—so we have at least half an hour to talk, as we always do, about the merchandise.

I look over her shoulder. "What's up?"

"I think I have a buyer for some of these," Carrie replies, "but he's trying to low-ball us. I'm checking out some online prices at eBay and Etsy. So far we're coming in much, much lower."

"I've got some trade publications here that will probably give you a better idea of their value. The prices on eBay and Etsy are over-inflated." I finally locate the antique price lists in a pile of magazines on a chair—when did I get this disorganized?—and hand them to Carrie.

"Here," I say, "check these out to make sure that I've priced the watches correctly."

I explain—probably for the umpteenth time—that I let things slide in the shop when my mother was ill and may not have adequately researched the prices. I vaguely recall that the watches were a box lot purchase I made at one of the few auctions in Ottawa I was able to attend before my mother became so ill.

Carrie takes the sheets I offer her. "He's a dick," she states categorically.

"Who are you talking about?" I ask, a bit taken aback by her language.

"Bob Corrigan," Carrie says without hesitation. "He relies on the fact that he's a longstanding customer who dates back to your parents' time. Have you noticed that he doesn't like to deal with me? He always asks for you."

But to be honest, I've never really noticed. I think of Bob as an old family friend: a link between the past and present. He's been buying antiques from my family as long as I can remember.

Is it possible I've become so consumed with thoughts of the mirror that I'm oblivious to everything else?

I'm no longer sure of myself.

Dear, practical Emily, where have you gone?

14

I had trouble falling asleep again last night, but I finally dozed off around midnight. I awoke around 3 AM to a banging sound downstairs in the shop. The sound was so loud that it rattled the windows of my bedroom.

I groped for my cellphone on my bedside table, flicked on the lamp, and dialled 911. After a brief conversation with the operator, she advised me that a police car was on its way and told me to stay in the apartment until I heard an officer knock at the shop door.

When the police arrived—it was fifteen minutes but the time seemed interminable—I ran downstairs to let them in. The noise had not abated: if anything, it had grown louder. It was coming from the backroom and sounded as if someone was repeatedly levelling blows with a gigantic sledge hammer.

"Is there another entrance to this place, miss?" one of the policemen asked.

"Yes, there's one that leads into the building from the alley."

"My partner and I will circle around back to see if the door's been jimmied." He had to almost scream over the noise.

"Don't open that door," he nodded to the door in the shop leading to the storage room, "until we've checked the back. In fact, it's probably best if you wait upstairs in your apartment."

"I'd rather stay here, but I'll keep my distance from the door."

He nodded and beckoned to his partner to accompany him outside. They were out there for about five minutes. When they returned, the officer who had done the talking thus far shook his head. "It's still locked. We'll try this door."

I silently handed him the key I'd taken from my desk.

"Stand back please, miss."

He opened the door with the key I'd given him while the other officer used his flashlight to find the light switch.

The banging abruptly stopped as light flooded the room.

There was no one there.

The officers circled the room, trying to identify the source of the noise, but they found nothing to account for the banging sound we'd all heard.

My eyes went instinctively to the dresser. They followed my gaze. On top of the dresser lay a razor-thin knife with blood clotted near the handle.

"Have you ever seen this knife?" the other officer, who had been quiet to this point, asked as he pulled on disposable gloves and placed it inside an evidence bag.

I shook my head.

"We'll have this run through our weapons ID database and also request a DNA test on the blood.

"Do you have anywhere else to stay tonight?"

"No, I'm okay, really, just a bit shaken. But I don't think you'll find that knife in your database."

"Why's that?"

"Because it's an antique. I can show you pictures of similar ones. You're looking at a weapon that dates back to the nineteenth century."

15

After the police left, I couldn't get back to sleep. I dressed and went downstairs to turn on my desk computer. I have another one upstairs that I use for personal finances, but the results of my previous searches were already recorded on the computer in the shop. I made myself a cup of tea, keeping a wary eye on the door to the backroom.

I had not viewed Edward in the mirror since this entity—whatever it was—had appeared to me. I assumed now that he was keeping Edward at bay, as if haunting him in death even as he had destroyed him in life.

I called up the database for the *Daily Telegraph* archives and began trying a number of keywords including "murder," "knife," and "Edward Fitzmorris." Edward's obituary appeared again, as well as the account of his murder. But there was also an article I hadn't seen before, dated two weeks after Edward's burial. I read it quickly. It was a follow-up on the police investigation into the murder stating that the police were still investigating, but currently had no suspects. I also learned that the attack occurred shortly after 6 PM and there were no witnesses on record. This was the fourth in a series of robberies/murders, and the police assumed the same assailant was involved. The similarities of the wounds on each of the victims had led them to this conclusion.

The murder weapon had not been recovered.

I suspected that this weapon was now in the custody of the Ottawa police.

16

When I next looked up to check the clock, it was almost 5 AM. I shut down my computer and scribbled a note for Carrie saying I'd be late coming into the shop because I hadn't slept well. I had no intention of telling her what had happened last night because I didn't want to alarm her. Besides, how could I rationally explain what was going on in the backroom? I barely believed it myself.

I went upstairs to my apartment, taking solace in its familiarity: the beautiful turn-of-the-nineteenth century armoire that my mother had lovingly refinished as a birthday gift for me; the antique, high-backed couch and matching chairs that I'd had re-upholstered; and the framed prints of pre-Raphaelite paintings I'd had since my university days. The one I loved the most was *The Lady of Shalott* by John William Waterhouse, who was not a member of the original pre-Raphaelites, but had adopted their style. I'd read Tennyson's poem in a Victorian English course at university and had found the print later in a small shop in Ottawa. I used to study it for hours, taking in the intricate details of the doomed heroine and her boat.

When I entered my bedroom, my eyes fell upon the framed portrait of my younger self—the one who smiled and believed anything was possible in life; the one who dreamed of exotic castles in the air.

When I picked up the photograph, I dislodged a small folded note. It said simply:

> I do not know you, but I have watched you from my mirror. I sense the kindred spirit of someone who has suffered great loss.

It was signed "Edward."

I'm beginning to doubt my own sanity. This can't be happening, but yet it is.

Where do I go from here?

17

It's almost noon when I come down the apartment stairs to the shop. Carrie is busy with a customer, but I manage to catch her eye so she knows I'm here. She casts me a worried look.

Once she rings up the sale of antique bookends, and the customer has left the store, she turns to me. "Are you okay? I've been worried about you."

"I'm fine. Just some noise last night. I think a cat knocked over the garbage cans in the alleyway," I lied, feeling guilty because I couldn't share the truth with her.

"Why don't you take the rest of the day off, Emily? I'll hold down the fort."

"Thanks for offering to look after things, Carrie. Actually, I haven't been out for a while, and I need to do some shopping. So yes, I'll take you up on your offer."

I grab my coat from the hall rack and start out the door.

A strange feeling comes over me as if, once I step across the threshold, I will be able to escape the hold the mirror exerts on me.

****

When I return from my shopping, I decide to try something. I'm anxious to know if I can reach Edward in the same manner he's been communicating with me.

I lock up the shop for the day after saying good-bye to Carrie and thanking her again for giving me the afternoon off. Then I sit at my desk and compose a note to Edward asking if he knows a way to drive his murderer's wicked spirit from the mirror.

I refuse to admit to myself how absurd this is. I don't know what else to do.

I unlock the door to the backroom and go to the dresser. Once again, the sheet has been displaced from the mirror, even though I've pinned it in place. I look down and see the safety pins scattered —useless—on the floor.

I start to insert the note in the frame of the mirror, when a malignant image fills it, beckoning menacingly at me.

I drop the note and run back inside the shop.

The phone is ringing on my desk. I grab it and say hello, out of breath.

"Hi, Miss Montfort. It's Detective Serge Lacroix from the Ottawa police. I hope I'm not calling at a bad time."

I reassure him that it's okay, and I'd be happy to speak to him.

"I'm just calling to update you on the knife our officers found in your backroom. There's nothing in our database to match it, and unfortunately the blood was too decomposed to do a DNA test. I'm sorry not to be of more help," he says apologetically, "but we'll make sure our patrol cars keep an eye on your shop. You might also want to install an alarm system in the room where the knife was found. I understand there's already one in the main part of your store."

I thank him and end the call. After all, how could I explain to him that the weapon was from a murder committed more than a century and a half ago and that I'd learned of this killing from a ghost?

18

I'm in the shop already when Carrie enters the next morning.

"Are you feeling any better, Emily?"

"Yes, thanks. I slept well last night." I'm waiting for my nose to grow like Pinocchio's.

"Can I talk to you for a minute, Emily?" she says quietly.

"Of course. Have a seat." I point to the empty chair across from my desk.

"I'm, er, worried about you. You don't seem to be yourself at all. I don't mean to intrude in your affairs, but I've noticed that you hardly interact with the customers any more. You spend most of your time at the computer. You're looking even paler than usual. And the stock is getting down. I'm sorry if I'm overstepping myself."

"It's okay, Carrie. I appreciate your concern, and you're right. I'm not sleeping well. And I've neglected my customers, and the stock *is* getting low. I'm afraid it's taken me longer than I expected to get over my mother's death, and I know that's not healthy. How about I go on a weekend buying trip? Can I leave the shop in your capable hands?"

"That sounds great, Emily." She hesitates and then pulls a business card from her purse. "I got this from my mom. It's the name of a grief counsellor she went to after my grandmother died."

I take the business card from her hand, genuinely touched by her concern. "Thanks, Carrie. I mean it. I appreciate your looking out for me. It means a lot to me."

She looks suddenly embarrassed and at a loss for words. I realize that she didn't expect me to take the card. She probably was bracing herself instead for a lecture on proper employer-employee relationships.

I ask impulsively, "Carrie, have you ever felt you belonged in another time?"

I'm mortified as soon as I say this, but to my relief, Carrie laughs. "Well, my mom always says that I should have been born in the '60s in the era of Woodstock. Why do you ask?"

"No reason, I'm just being silly."

I leave the conversation there, half regretful that I didn't confide in her.

19

It's the weekend, and as promised, I've left Carrie in charge of the shop and am travelling the back roads again to find additional stock. I've made a list of auctions and estate sales, and I've decided to stay overnight at a bed and breakfast near Smiths Falls. This will give me a chance to work all of the sales on Saturday and then start fresh again on Sunday.

I drive to the first estate sale, which is using the same auction service as the one from which I purchased the dresser. I'm early, and I walk around the yard where all of the goods are displayed. This time the owners have not died, but have moved into an apartment and are selling most of their belongings. The house itself is also up for auction. It's a lovely old stone house with latticed windows, and the grounds have been meticulously maintained so I'm hoping it will fetch a good price for them.

I nod at other people I know from previous sales, and exchange small talk. It's hot this morning and the mosquitoes are out in full force. I swat them away from my face as I talk, and someone kindly hands me a can of bug spray. I apply a liberal dose and return it to its owner. He smiles shyly at me, an elderly man bent over a cane, and says, "Weapon of choice in this neck of the woods." I laugh and realize how nice it is to be on a buying trip again.

I've had a call from a small movie company who'll be filming in Ottawa in two months. They want to rent antiques for their late nineteenth-century set so I'm looking for andirons, brass candlesticks, lacework, period-piece furniture and dishes, and a host of other antiques. I've already spotted some items to buy.

I've gone to the house to register and get my number for bidding, and now I'm doing a second circuit of the furniture in the yard. I mentally check off the things I want to bid on: there's a beautiful Edwardian china cabinet with matching table and chairs; several oil paintings of nature scenes that would fit into the movie set; a child's rocking chair;

a milking stool; some antique embroidery and china; and several old kerosene lamps. All in all, a very good selection. I unfold the lawn chair I've brought with me and wait for the auction to begin.

Within an hour, the auctioneer jumps up on the wagon that will serve as his base of operations; tests his microphone; and briefly outlines the terms of the auction. He begins with some box lots of small appliances; radios; wall clocks; and miscellaneous linens and dishes. Quite often these items are left to the end of an auction, but he wants to clear these out first because they're crowding his space on the wagon and he needs more room to move. He goes on from there to various outdoor machinery and implements and then to the larger furniture items. I've been daydreaming, but I become alert as he moves to the china cabinet, table, and chairs, which he announces will be sold as a set. The bidding is brisk, but finally it's down to two of us, the other person I recognize as an Ottawa antique dealer. I already have a buyer lined up for this set so I keep bidding, and finally the dealer calls it quits, doffs his hat and bows to me, and I smile and wave at him in return.

I'm feeling more contented now than I have in a long time. It's the combination of the wonderful weather, the good-natured grumbling of the auctioneer about the heat and bugs as he swigs from his bottle of water, and the general camaraderie of the setting.

At noon I grab a sandwich from the canteen and wait for the auction to resume. By the end of the day, I'm exhausted, but I've managed to get most of the items I wanted, and I've already called Ed Scott to arrange their delivery to Ottawa.

As I fold up my chair and prepare to take my small purchases to the car, I see the auctioneer making his way toward me. "Hi, it's Emily, isn't it? My dad spotted you earlier. He had to leave for another auction, but he wanted me to tell you how sorry he was to hear about your mom. She and your father apparently used to attend all of his auctions."

I shake his hand and thank him. "By the way, I bought a tiger stripe dresser from you at that estate auction for the Cunninghams a couple of months back."

His face clouds over. "Funny about that piece. The son told me it belonged to his great-uncle who'd been murdered in England, and his grandmother refused to part with it and brought it over to Canada with her. His mother kept it in a spare bedroom. He hinted there were some old wives' tales about it being haunted. He said he was glad to be rid of it. It always gave him the creeps."

20

I'm soaking in the antique claw foot tub at the B&B and thinking over what the auctioneer said to me about the dresser. At least now I know that it has a history, and even if the stories have been written off as old wives' tales, there have been others before me who saw things in the mirror. I'm not sure if this makes me feel better or worse.

I dry myself off, change into my pyjamas and robe, grab a book, and settle on the bed, which is soft and comfortable. I've already had a late supper at a nearby restaurant.

I find myself dozing off around 9 PM.

I awake, terrified, to the memory of a nightmare in which a man with a knife has me cornered in the backroom of my shop, and I'm unable to move or scream for help.

21

I spend Sunday at more auctions and although I make some purchases, my heart's not really in it. I'm still upset from the nightmare. I'm unable to shake this feeling of doom.

When I return to the shop late that afternoon, I retrieve the business card Carrie has given me. I've decided I need outside help.

I leave a message on the doctor's answering machine asking for a return call next business day and try, without success, to tell myself that everything will be all right.

22

It's Monday and I'm heading for the backroom to wait for Ed Scott to deliver my weekend purchases.

When I open the door, I find the note to Edward that I dropped on the floor last week. Impulsively, I tuck it into the frame of the mirror, which reveals nothing to me except my pale reflection.

I hear Ed's truck out in the alleyway and open the outer door for him. It takes his crew almost an hour to unload everything in the space I've cleared. I pay him and thank him and his helpers.

Carrie comes out to see the furniture I've purchased.

"What a gorgeous set," she exclaims as she spots the matching table, chairs, and china cabinet.

"I've got a customer, Mrs. Garrett, who's been looking for a set like this for a long time for her dining room. I think she'll like it. I'll give her a call later," I tell Carrie, as she examines my other purchases.

She beams at me with that wonderful smile of hers and says, "Wow, great job. Looks like you've got most of the items on the list the movie company gave you."

We hear the bell over the front door ring, and Carrie hurries off to see to the customer.

I'm almost finished making an inventory of the new items when I notice that the note has come dislodged from the mirror. I stoop down to pick it up and when I straighten, there's a clamminess in the room that wasn't there before.

I glance in the mirror and see a black fog that suddenly shifts its shape into a man whose features are hidden by a hood. Before I can scream, the tentacles of fog become hands that wrap themselves around my neck.

The pressure is overwhelming: I can't get my breath.

It's squeezing the life out of me.

I can't wrench its hands from my neck.

23

The next thing I remember is Carrie standing over me looking frightened to death. "God, Emily, what happened? I think I should call an ambulance."

I sit up with her help and ask for a cold cloth. "Don't call an ambulance, Carrie." What the hell would I tell them: that I was strangled by fog? "I'm okay, honestly. I must have fainted, is all. I haven't been eating well, and I skipped breakfast. Help me to my desk and you can make me a cup of tea. I think I have some crackers there."

She looks doubtful, but helps pull me to my feet. I lean against her as we make our way into the shop, and she seats me at my desk and starts rummaging through the drawers. She finds some packaged cheese and crackers, and opens them for me.

I touch her arm to reassure her I'm okay. She leaves my side reluctantly to plug in the electric kettle for tea. When she returns she fusses over me. "God, Emily, I felt so helpless when I found you. I've never had to deal with anything like this before."

"It's okay, Carrie. You did exactly what was needed."

I see her looking at my neck.

"Christ, Emily, what are those red welts?"

I momentarily panic, wondering what on earth I can say that will sound plausible. I realize I'm wearing a neck scarf and that gives me an idea. I tug the scarf from my neck and say, "I think it's from my scarf. I must have held onto it too tightly before I fainted and it left marks on my neck."

She looks at me incredulously, starts to speak and then decides against it, and turns away to make me a cup of tea.

24

It's Wednesday and I'm sitting in the grief counsellor's waiting room, reading a year-old *Maclean's* magazine and wondering why on earth I've come here.

The receptionist calls my name and beckons toward a doorway. "You can go in now."

A pleasant-faced woman in her mid-fifties ushers me into her office and tells me she is Dr. Stewart. "Come in, Emily. I see this is your first appointment with me." She gestures to a comfortable-looking leather chair.

Once I'm seated, she tells me that the first appointment is a chance to get comfortable with one another, and she doesn't want me to feel pressured.

"Can you tell me a bit about yourself, Emily?"

I talk about the antique shop that I've inherited, explaining that my father died of a heart attack more than ten years ago and that my mother died of Alzheimer's disease several months ago.

"Do you feel like talking to me about your father's death, Emily?"

I'm surprised by the question, expecting that she would focus on my mother. "When my dad died, it was very sudden. He'd been diagnosed with high blood pressure, but my mother and I never expected a heart attack."

"It's been quite a while, but do you remember how you coped with his death?"

"I was in my first year of university, then, at Ottawa U. I remember getting the call from my mother at the hospital: she told me Dad had gone into cardiac arrest. I'd never heard that emptiness in her voice before. She was a few years older than Dad and had always joked about being the first to go. I don't think she ever thought that he would die before her."

"How did you feel when your father died, Emily?"

"It was so sudden that I guess I was in denial for a while. It wasn't really until the funeral that I realized he was never coming back. He was a wonderful father. He was always taciturn with others, and some people mistook this as an uncaring attitude. But those who knew him also realized how deeply he cared for his family.

"He tried to be a disciplinarian when I was growing up, but it just wasn't in him. I was always his little princess, and he spoiled me. I guess what I appreciated the most about him was that he was always proud of me and made a special effort to celebrate my accomplishments—both of my parents did—so my Grade Eight and high school graduations were major events. He was so proud of me when I went to university." I hesitate, unable to go on, because my dad was not there for my university graduation.

"Let's stop here for the day, Emily. I hope you'll continue with your appointments. Shall I ask my receptionist to set up another one? Is the same time next week best for you?"

25

By the fourth appointment, I was beginning to feel I could trust Dr. Stewart and confide in her. She'd filled me in on her background, having previously been a counsellor for victims of domestic abuse.

"I see the same pattern of grief in those I counsel," she'd told me. "In one case, it's the grief of someone who's lost the love of their partner and often their hope for a future life. It's easy for us to think that shelters will care for battered women but in many cases they see no viable option for their future, especially when they have children. They've become totally dependent financially and often emotionally on their abusers.

"In the case of a person who's suffered the death of a loved one, there are similar signs of withdrawal and fear of the future. The self-help industry writes about the five stages of grief, but the reality is that each person responds to grief differently, and we can't compartmentalize these emotions."

At this meeting, I was finally able to confront my mom's death.

Dr. Stewart said something to me that I hadn't really thought about before. "The loss of a loved one to Alzheimer's disease is a double loss. There's the grieving for the person who died, but there's also a grieving for the person we once knew. It's such an extended process because the grieving for the person who once was begins almost as soon as Alzheimer's disease is diagnosed. In many cases this grieving can last three to six years or as long as the person lives. You had three years of grieving before your mother died, Emily, and not just the several months since her death. It's important you recognize this fact. Can you describe to me how you felt during those three years that you were your mother's caregiver?"

I thought about it for a long time before replying. "My mom used to call our family 'The Three Musketeers'. After Dad died, I still had my mom, but when she was diagnosed with Alzheimer's disease, I knew that I was truly alone. If I'm honest, there was a lot of self-pity: feelings of abandonment. Toward the end, I'd resigned myself to the fact of her death, I guess, but I had trouble seeing any future for myself without her."

"From what you've told me of your mother, she'd be the first person to 'forgive' you for letting her go."

"You're right, but it seems like such a betrayal."

"Imagine that she's standing in front of you right now, Emily. What would you say to her?"

I closed my eyes and tried to imagine my mother standing before me—not as she was when she died, but as the vibrant person I once knew.

I started weeping openly, but for once I didn't care. I was beyond keeping up appearances. I blurted out, "Why did you have to leave me alone, Mom, why?"

Dr. Stewart gave me a few moments and then said, "The hardest part of being someone's child is accepting that your parents won't always be there—that they're mortal. But everyone dies, Emily, that's the sad truth of life. That doesn't negate everything that person accomplished in life, the things you hold dear to you. It's not a disloyalty to your mom to accept the fact of her death."

****

Later that evening as I was about to fall asleep in my apartment, I felt a presence beside me on the bed. I knew instinctively that it was my mother. She stroked my hair as she did when I was a child and she wanted to comfort me.

Of course, I'd been preparing myself for this because Dr. Stewart explained to me that hallucinations are fairly common in the grieving process. She said that the mind tricks us into believing we see the loved one we've lost.

But my mother seemed so real to me that I was disoriented and breathless.

I tried to relax my breathing.

I understood that she'd come here for a purpose: to reassure me that it was okay to let her go.

26

I've finally had to face my grief openly and acknowledge the fact of my mother's death. I'm hoping that I can move on. I'm actually feeling better now. Stronger. I'm taking more interest in the day-to-day operations of the shop, and I even had a discreet word with Bob Corrigan, the man who—as Carrie pointed out—was trying to take advantage of his friendship with my parents to undercut prices. I did it as tactfully as I could, drawing up a price list with a notation at the top that said, "Please note that prices are non-negotiable." I gave a copy to Mr. Corrigan when I saw him in the store, saying, "We have a new price list now. It makes it easier for Carrie and me. This way, customers won't feel the need to barter." His face blanched when I said this, and I'm not sure if he'll be back, but Carrie was delighted that I'd supported her.

I've been able to attract a lot of new customers through word of mouth. The movie company to which I'd rented antiques was happy with my finds, and as a result I've had other small companies approach me for props. In addition, Carrie has come up with the idea of holding a clinic each Tuesday, which is usually a slow day. It's a similar idea to the *Antiques Roadshow*: people bring in their antiques for free appraisal. It's not only allowed me to find some treasured pieces—those that people are willing to sell—but has also expanded my customer base. Once again, I think how lucky I was to hire Carrie. She's full of new ideas for the store.

Although I trusted Dr. Stewart, I didn't raise the subject of the mirror. I guess I was afraid of her reaction. Afraid that she'd think I wasn't making progress.

But when I allow myself to think of the mirror, I can't just dismiss my experiences. How do I explain the images in the mirror, the noise in the backroom, the mangled tintype, the bloody knife, and my attempted strangling? The note I received in my bedroom from Edward has now mysteriously disappeared, but I know it was real, and I've committed its words to memory.

No, I'm not quite ready to write off these incidents as hallucinations.

I haven't been in the backroom for a month, except to replenish stock, and then I always take Carrie with me, ostensibly to help me carry out the items.

I think I'm ready to go back now. I feel strong enough to confront the demon that is threatening Edward.

27

I've been doing research these past few weeks on mirrors as portals for dead spirits to re-enter the world, and I've discovered that this belief is shared by many cultures, some of which choose to drape mirrors with sheets after a death in the family to avoid entrapment of the soul of their loved one. Up until the time the dresser entered my shop, I would have scoffed at such a notion, but I can no longer dismiss it as mere superstition.

I've also learned that evil spirits prey on strong emotions, which means that my grief may have attracted the spirit of Edward's killer.

My theory is that because the murderer of Edward was never identified or captured, his spirit roams freely in the other world.

I can't believe I'm saying this, but then again it's difficult to believe anything that's happened to me the past few months.

I believe that if I can somehow dispel the spirit of this entity, I can be rid of it.

****

I've tried several suggested remedies over the past few days, including candles, incense, and amethyst crystals. None of these items has worked. When I go back there, an unmistakable chill hangs in the air and there's a stench of decay that I hadn't noticed before when Carrie and I were in the room.

I'm beginning to despair that I'll ever cast out this evil. I'm wondering if I should just smash the mirror into pieces and bury the shards. At least then, it would have no further hold over me. But what would become of Edward? Would I be freeing his soul or consigning him to an existence in limbo?

28

As a last resort, I search the internet again to find something that could help me. Finally, I happen upon a site that includes a list of mirror spells, and suggests using a small round mirror and painting the back of it black. The mirror is supposed to act as a portal to disperse the evil into space where it will be destroyed.

I've prepared the mirror and am now entering the backroom where I will hang it high on the opposite wall near the ceiling as the site recommends.

As I climb the ladder, a stench of rotten flesh fills the room, and it begins to shake under me.

I grab a nearby bookcase to steady myself and, despite my trembling hands, I'm finally able to place the mirror on the wall.

I see tendrils of the black fog that almost strangled the life out of me several weeks ago. This time, however, it is drawn to the mirror I've positioned on the wall. I try to remember the next steps in the spell, and then I realize that I must picture a door in the centre of the glass: it will allow the evil spirit to enter the mirror, but never to return. Then, as a final step, I draw the sign of the cross on the glass surface.

There's an unearthly scream as the black fog dissipates in the mirror.

It's working!

29

I must leave the mirror in place for seven days and then take it down and use vinegar to remove any residue of negative energy that clings to it.

Today is the seventh day. I haven't entered the backroom since the night I hung the mirror so it's with trepidation that I unlock the door and switch on the light. The mirror is there, reflecting nothing because of the height at which I needed to hang it.

I pull over the ladder, climbing it slowly, step by step. I'm about to reach for the mirror when I hear a loud clattering noise below me. My heart racing, I finally realize that it is only a small hammer that has fallen because I've forgotten to remove it from a rung of the ladder.

My hand reaches for the mirror, and

I pull it from the wall. Steeling myself, I glance into it, but see nothing except my own frightened face.

I dismount the ladder and take the mirror to the kitchen to wash it.

****

It's later in the evening, and I've gone back several times to see if I can spot Edward in the dresser mirror, but there is nothing there. I fear I may have trapped his soul, as well as the evil spirit, in the second mirror.

The thought makes me so sad that I hang my head to cry.

30

It's been two months now since I last glimpsed Edward, and I'm beginning to accept the fact that his spirit has either been destroyed or has returned to his other world.

Carrie and I are very busy in the shop. It's nearing Christmas, and clients are either buying antiques for their homes, or purchasing them as gifts.

It snowed heavily today, which always brings out the shoppers. It will be the first Christmas I've spent without my mother. Carrie has invited me to her parents' house in the country where she assures me that her brothers and sisters and the grandchildren will make it so chaotic and fun that I'll never have time to catch my breath. I'm actually considering it, although I've told Carrie I'll get back to her.

A white-haired woman enters the shop and stamps her feet on the inside mat. Her cheeks are red from the cold, and her hair is covered with a fine mist of melting snow. She laughs. "I feel like Santa Claus."

It's only then that I realize it's Dr. Stewart. "Come in, come in. I didn't recognize you with all the snow." I ask her if she'd like a cup of tea to warm herself up.

"How are you doing, Emily? This isn't the happiest time of year for a lot of people," she says, as I take her coat and let her settle in the chair opposite my desk.

"All in all, I think I'm coping much better. I'm not turning cartwheels, but I feel more at peace with myself than I have for a long while."

"I'm so happy to hear that. When you left the last session, I wasn't sure if you planned to continue with the therapy. When my receptionist didn't hear from you, I assumed that you felt you didn't need more sessions. Is that the case?"

I'm embarrassed now that I didn't get back to Dr. Stewart or her receptionist to let them know I was doing well. I tell her this.

"Oh, don't worry about it, Emily. I knew you owned this shop and decided to pop by and say hello. I'm pleased that you're doing well. I think you have more colour in your face now, and you seem more animated to me. Those are both very good signs.

"I also stopped in because I'm looking for an antique cameo brooch for my sister."

After she's finished her tea, I lead her over to a black velvet display case with antique jewellery. I have several cameos in stock because I love their intricate design.

Dr. Stewart picks up one of my favourites: a large jet stone with the silhouette of a young woman encased in a filigree brass setting. She asks me the provenance of the brooch, and I tell her that an elderly woman brought it in one day. She'd acquired it in an estate sale, but told me she thought she'd never wear it.

"It's beautiful, Emily," Dr. Stewart says as she glances at the price tag, "and very reasonably priced. I'm sure my sister will love it."

"I'll gift wrap it for you, Dr. Stewart."

I hand the box to her after I've wrapped it in gift paper and added a bow. As I ring up the sale, she smiles at me. "I've always suspected that you were keeping something from me, Emily. Something—or someone—capable of making you feel happy again. Never be afraid to spread your wings."

Funny, I think, as she leaves the shop.

That's exactly something Mom would have said to me.

31

I accepted Carrie's invitation to spend Christmas with her family and was glad I did. She was right that there was total chaos in the house, but I didn't mind. It was just what I needed. I laughed myself silly at the antics of the grandchildren. They were dressed angelically in velvet outfits, but every time I looked, one of them had shed a shoe or sock or had managed to dribble chocolate or smear markers on their clothes. They cheered when their mothers finally gave up and let them change into overalls once the family pictures had been taken.

Carrie's father dropped me off at my apartment later, telling me on the way how happy his daughter's been since she started working for me. I tell him that she's been wonderful for me too and a great asset for the store.

The shop windows are decorated with twinkling white lights—Carrie calls them fairy lights—and look quite festive. I unlock the shop door and then go upstairs to my apartment. Carrie's mother has sent me a huge basket of food that will keep me stuffed for a week. After I put everything away in the fridge, I pour a glass of Bailey's—a gift from Carrie—and move into the living room. I turn on the gas fireplace, as well as the lights of the small Christmas tree I've placed on the window seat overlooking the street.

I sigh. I haven't felt this peaceful in a long time.

As I sip my drink, my eyes fall on a paper-wrapped box that I've never seen before. It's under my Christmas tree, but I'm sure it wasn't there when I turned on the lights earlier.

A glimmer of hope rises in my chest as I unwrap the box.

Yes, it is indeed from Edward! There's a note with an inscription from Matthew Arnold's *Dover Beach*. "Ah, love, let us be true/To one another." Inside the box is a strand of beautiful white pearls.

I run quickly downstairs and unlock the backroom door. I sit before the mirror wearing the pearls Edward has given me. He is in the mirror once again. I place my hand against his. I cannot reach him, but I know he is there for me.

Edward tells me through his gestures that the spirit of his murderer has been cast away forever, but, as I feared, his spirit was also dispersed. It has taken him this long to make his way back to me.

32

The next two months pass in a blur. I've given Carrie the time off to spend with her family and join friends at a ski resort in Vermont because sales are typically slow during this post-Christmas period. She's due back at the end of this week. I've missed her smile and her chatter: my surrogate little sister.

I've spent most of my time sitting in front of the mirror conversing with Edward. We can't really talk to one another, but miraculously we're able to exchange notes—which I find all over the shop and my apartment. At first, this seemed to be such an artificial form of communication, but now it's second nature to me. The wonderful thing about the act of writing is that you do not lie: instead, you lay your soul bare.

I've managed to piece together Edward's life story before the murder. He was a physician in London who cared for injured factory workers. He had a small inheritance from his father and with it, he was able to establish an agency that tried to get children off the streets and find them good homes so they could attend school.

He told me he was returning from a visit to one of his patients when he was attacked by his murderer.

It's sad to me that he's only a footnote in history because of his murder. He deserved so much more. He has a kindness and nobility that I've come to admire deeply. Sensing this about him, I finally summon the courage to leave him a special note to tell him what I think he's been waiting to hear: *I love you*. When he reads these words, the veil of sorrow lifts from his eyes, as if the shadow of death no longer imprisons him.

I've had relationships before, but ironically I've never felt this close to anyone. I'm constantly frightened that this won't last: that it will indeed turn out to be a hallucination.

I'm also afraid that the mirror is only a one-way portal, and I will never be able to reach him. I've examined every inch of it—front and back—but in the end it's an ordinary mirror with wooden slats in the back to hold it in place and bolts to attach it to the frame above the dresser.

But Edward assures me that when the moment is right, the mirror will become porous so I can pass over to him.

33

Edward looks particularly serious and almost nervous today. I'm wondering if he thinks that once Carrie returns, I'll no longer have time for him.

He finally gestures with his hand to the top drawer of the dresser. Inside there is a note:

> I have left you something in your apartment, Emily. I hope I have not been too presumptuous.

I run upstairs to my bedroom. There on my bed is a beautiful white satin and lace gown and a wreath of orange blossoms, their scent permeating the air.

I finger the material in the gown and realize that it's to be my wedding dress.

I will need just a few days to put my

affairs in order.

34

I've left a note for Carrie telling her that I'm travelling aboard and asking her to take charge of the shop. She'll be suspicious, of course, but I'm not really lying to her. I know that if I choose to enter the mirror, I will be away for a long time. In fact there may be no way for me to return.

But I mustn't think of this now. For once, I must not question my motives ... I must not analyze things to death.

I pick up the beautiful white gown that Edward has left for me.

I slip the dress over my head and fasten the pearl necklace he's given me. In my bedroom mirror, I view my reflection. The gown flows perfectly.

I loosen my hair, let it fall around my shoulders, and don the bridal wreath of orange blossoms. For once, I feel almost beautiful.

I walk downstairs to the backroom and sit before the mirror.

He is there waiting for me.

He holds out his hand.

I reach into the mirror, which is suddenly porous as he said it would be, and take it.

And then I step through the mirror.

I'm uncertain whether I'm going to my wedding or to my death.

35

It's almost 9 AM, and Carrie's bus has been late once again. She curses under her breath as she unlocks the shop door.

She calls out for Emily but there is no response. *She must be sleeping in.*

Carrie flips over the closed sign on the door, tidies the front counter, and checks the float in the cash drawer.

The bell over the door rings, and the first customer of the day enters.

****

It's been a very busy morning for this time of year, and when Carrie glances at the metal school clock above the desk, she sees that it's almost 10:30 AM and still no sign of Emily. Now she is starting to worry. She places a handwritten "back in five minutes" note on the door and runs up the stairs to Emily's apartment. There's no answer when she calls her name and knocks repeatedly.

Carrie races down to the shop again to find the spare key that Emily leaves in the desk. She pointed it out to Carrie one day and told her to use it in case of an emergency. Emily probably had in mind a fire or pipes bursting, but Carrie decides this *is* an emergency. Emily's car is parked out back, but there's still no sign of her.

As the apartment door opens, she calls out Emily's name once again, but there is no answer. The apartment itself is immaculate—as Carrie had pictured it—and as she moves into the living room, she sees it's furnished with lovely antiques and prints which Emily has no doubt carefully chosen. She finds the bedroom: the door is open and the bed is made. She's about to leave the room when she spots an envelope with her name propped up against a picture of a young and smiling Emily on the corner desk. Carrie takes the envelope and locks up the apartment. Having been out of the shop for at least fifteen minutes, she decides to take it downstairs to open.

She reads the letter as she sits behind the front counter, keeping an eye out for customers.

Dear Carrie,

This will seem totally out of character for someone like me, but I had a last minute opportunity to travel abroad and decided it was what I needed. It's been so long since I've done anything but work, and I think a vacation is in order. I'm not sure how long I'll be away, but I expect that it will be for a few months at least.

I hope you'll be able to work full time in the store. If you want to hire someone else to help you, I've planned ahead and had my lawyer draw up a power of attorney so you'll have access to my business account. His name's Coulter, and he'll be contacting you in a couple of days. He's a stiff upper lip type, but he's very trustworthy. I've also left a list of contacts who can help you out when the stock is running low. They keep track of auctions and the like, and they may have some of their own stock that they'll sell you at reasonable prices.

I don't know if I've thanked you enough for all the help you've given me since you started working here. Probably not, so I will say it now. Thank you so much. I consider you a dear friend, almost like my little sister!

Please forgive my impulsiveness and wish me well.

Love,

Emily

Carrie re-reads the note, and still it doesn't feel right.

This isn't the Emily I know—the one who plans ahead for weeks at a time and makes post-it notes to remind herself of appointments.

And signing over the store to me, that makes no sense. She's known me for less than a year. Who puts that kind of trust in another person?

36

Carrie has managed to catch an express bus this morning so for once she is early, half expecting to see Emily when she opens the shop door. Part of her still doesn't believe that she'd leave so precipitously. But the shop is empty. She turns on the lights and prepares for another day of business, wondering for the millionth time since she read Emily's letter what has really happened to her.

The phone rings around 10 AM, and it's the lawyer asking if he can stop by with some papers. Carrie readily agrees to meet with him, thinking maybe she'll get more information about Emily's sudden departure.

He arrives an hour later, and they shake hands and exchange pleasantries. He's an older man, probably late sixties, with a thatch of white hair and a back that's as stiff as an ironing board.

Coulter looks uncomfortable and displeased as he hands Carrie the power of attorney form that Emily has signed.

"Do you have any idea where she's gone? Did she leave you a forwarding address or phone number?" she asks him.

His face wrinkles into the semblance of a prune. "No, and it's highly unusual. She called me a couple of days ago and told me what she wanted to do. I of course advised her against the power of attorney, no offence to you, miss, but as her lawyer I need to look out for her interests. She wouldn't be dissuaded, however, so I drew up the papers, and she signed them and dropped them off at my office. That was Wednesday, I believe." He consults the electronic schedule on his cellphone and nods absently. "She said she was going to Europe and would send me her coordinates shortly. I've had no contact with her since then."

He points to the power of attorney form and a separate bundle of documents. "These are her latest bank records for the business. I think that's everything you'll need, but you're welcome to contact me at any time if you have questions."

He starts to leave and then stops abruptly to pose a final question: "How old are you, miss, if you can pardon my asking?"

Obviously Emily's trust in Carrie is not shared by her lawyer, but then she can't really blame him.

This is insane, Emily. Where are you?

37

It's been almost three months since Emily left.

Carrie has been doing very well with the shop in spite of her initial qualms about taking over. Her mother has been a wonderful help: she's retired and is working in the store part time. She's in her element, of course, surrounded by antiques, and even refuses to let her daughter pay her. In addition, Carrie's parents have been going on weekend junkets to help her replenish the stock. They both enjoy being able to buy items without the residual guilt, knowing that the antiques will go to the shop rather than to their own hobby farm where the outbuildings are already stacked high with furniture.

Her mother is watching the shop so

Carrie decides she'll check out the back storeroom. Unfortunately, she hasn't had a chance to look there since Emily left, and wants to do an inventory of what items she can repair herself before asking for outside assistance. Emily may be gone, but Carrie is guarding her bottom line for her return.

The tiger stripe dresser immediately catches her eye, and she notices that Emily never got around to removing the water stain on its surface. The hinges of the mirror seem to be loose, and as she reaches up to tighten the bolts, she sees a sudden flash of dark hair in the mirror.

She screams, and her mother is quickly beside her. Her face is contorted with worry. "What is it, Carrie? What on earth happened?" She looks uneasily around the room.

Carrie points to the mirror, but there is nothing to see now except their two reflections.

"I know where Emily is, Mom. You've got to believe me! I know what I saw. Emily's inside the mirror."

38

I've been so happy here that time itself has lost its relevance. I spend each day with Edward walking the streets of London, attending trade union and social reform meetings in the back streets far away from the prying eyes of the police, and visiting book shops and small art galleries. At first I was terrified by the sheer mass of people in this city, but Edward reassured me that we are both unfettered by flesh and can move about unnoticed. Only occasionally do I encounter someone with the prescience to sense our spirits.

We live in a modest house with antiques that are still in their youth, and we talk at length, although we dare not plan a future.

At night we sit by lamplight and read. He loves to have me read aloud to him. Tonight

I'm reading from Emily Bronte's *Wuthering Heights*. Edward is not familiar with the name of the author because the novel was published under the male pseudonym Ellis Bell, but he readily accepts the fact that a woman could have written with such strength and passion. Despite the age in which he lives, he treats me as an equal.

I've decided I'm not going back to my old life. My time is no longer out of joint: I have found the century to which I truly belong. I don't know how much longer I will be blessed to stay by Edward's side, but I will remain here as long as I can. I understand that he is a ghost, but he is more substantial to me than any man I've ever known.

My one regret is that I had to leave without saying good-bye to Carrie. I keep appearing in the mirror to reassure her that I'm okay, but she's seldom in the backroom. I thought I saw her the other day, but I'm not sure if I was visible to her. I'll keep trying, though, to reach her. I won't give up.

I've been sharing memories of my mother with Edward. Surprisingly, there are many happy stories I now remember, and he laughs as I tell him how comical she could be.

I'm also keeping a daily journal. Perhaps, someday, someone else will walk through the portal of the mirror. They will see there's nothing at all to fear when they read the account of my redemption.

Acknowledgments

As always, I'd like to thank my husband Mike McCann for encouraging me to continue writing and for all the work he did to ready this book for publication. Thanks, Mike, for your support. It really means a lot.

I'd also like to thank my readers, Margaret Leroux and Katherine Hooton, for taking the time to review the manuscript and offer their suggestions for improvement.

"The Portal" has its basis in a true story. A work colleague of mine purchased an old dresser, and he and his girlfriend immediately started seeing an elderly lady, who was always weeping, in the attached mirror. I know that both of them were deeply saddened by this image, and I have no reason at all to doubt their veracity.

The tiger stripe dresser in this story is modelled on one that my maternal grandmother, Jean Birmingham, owned. It was passed down through the family. The water stain post-dates my grandmother's death. (She would have been mortified by the stain because she kept all of her belongings in pristine condition.)

This novella allowed me the pleasure of writing about two of my favourite subjects: antiques and the Victorian era. If you'd like to learn more about some of the antiques mentioned in the story, please see the following: https://en.wikipedia.org/ wiki/Post-mortem_photography; https://en.wikipedia.org/wiki/Tintype (post mortem and tintype photography); https://en.wikipedia.org/wiki/Magic_lantern (magic lanterns); https://en.wikipedia.org/wiki/ Box_camera (box cameras); https://www.leaf.tv/ articles/ how-to-identify-an-antique-cameo (cameos); and https://www.pinterest.com.au/ junekellam/tiger-oak/?autologin=true (tiger stripe furniture).

For Victorian culture, politics, art, and literature, as well as many additional subjects, see http://victorianweb.org/ index.html. For bridal wear and flowers, I have referred to http://www.victoriaspast.com/VictorianWedding2/bride.htm.

A list of the top ten British genealogical websites is available at https://www.thoughtco.com/top-databases-for-british-genealogy-1422740. The *Daily Telegraph* of Britain was founded in 1855 as the *Daily Telegraph and Courier*. Its newspaper archives go back more than four hundred years and include births, deaths, marriages, arrest records, and murder cases:

https://newspaperarchive.com/uk/.

There are numerous resources on mirrors as portals, including http://www.psychicsuniverse. com/articles/spirituality/living-spiritual-life/ rituals/mirrors-and-spirit-realm-legend-and-lore; and http://thesearchergroup.ca/mirrors/.

There are also many articles on banishing evil spirits, including an 11-step wikiHow on ridding oneself of demons: https://www.wikihow.com/ Get-Rid-of-Demons. The source I consulted for the use of the second mirror to trap the evil spirit is found at http://www.angelfire.com/ bc/ KensGodRules/Celtic/Doc/Mirror.html.

This story is dedicated to my mother-in-law, Janet McCann, who has lived with Alzheimer's disease for the past eight years.

The Experiment

In memory of my father-in-law,
Hugh Dominic McCann,
a very special man.

1

My name is Jack Booth, and I share this story with five other people. The six of us have extra-sensory abilities.

In my case, I'm an empath. My mother Marilyn once told me that my *condition* started when I was three. I'd be playing quietly and then all of a sudden cover my ears and start shaking my head. Sometimes I'd cry; other times I'd scream.

Alarmed by my behaviour, my mother dragged me to doctor after doctor, each doing a battery of tests and finding nothing. The last of these general practitioners recommended a child psychiatrist. Of course, my mother put her foot down at this suggestion. No self-respecting member of her family had ever seen a psychiatrist, and she equated this field of medicine with quackery.

My father was a very quiet man who never questioned my mother's pronouncements on my *abnormality*, as she called it. He had married her in his early twenties in a moment of optimism that clearly had faded with each passing day. He hid behind his newspaper when not at work, trying to avoid contact with both of us. Occasionally he would fix me with a baleful stare and sigh, as if wishing that I could measure up to my mother's expectations so there would be some peace and quiet in the house.

My father died when I was twelve. I always thought of it as my dad's Great Escape from the two of us. If there's an afterlife, maybe Dad's finally getting that peace and quiet.

By high school, I had learned—more or less—to compartmentalize the feelings I sensed from others so I could still function without those emotions overwhelming me. In fact, I hid my talents well. I was largely invisible to the other students in my school: too average in their estimation to be popular, but not worth bullying when there were so many other obvious targets.

My mother died when I was in the last

year of high school. Her funeral was a very sensible affair, having proceeded according to the written instructions she left behind. Staring at her coffin before it was lowered into the ground, I recognized the irony of constantly being overwhelmed by the feelings of others while I myself had so little emotional attachment to either of my parents, other than residual guilt for not measuring up to their idea of a good son.

It was when I went to university that I encountered Derek Avery, who would change the course of my life forever.

2

Derek Avery, a failed PhD student who nevertheless presented himself as *Dr.* Avery, had created a false resume that no one had ever bothered to verify. He'd managed to ingratiate himself with a group of academics who were genuinely interested in researching the brain's capacity for growth. Derek had a chameleon-like ability to adapt to any social circle and to give the outward appearance of caring greatly for the future of humanity. In reality, the only future he cared about was his own, and the only research he was interested in was how to make more money. Morality never entered into the equation for him.

Derek's parents had both been in their forties when he was born, and they'd loved their only child dearly. They were the owners of one of the very few mom-and pop-stores still left in Ottawa and had always scrambled to make ends meet. They'd hoped that their son would some day take over their business, but from an early age, Derek had displayed little interest in it. In fact, he had been embarrassed by what he thought of as its "lowliness" and he never brought his friends there, telling them instead that his parents both worked for one of Ottawa's largest legal firms. When he went to university, he never looked back, only contacting his parents when he needed money, which they readily provided even though it involved great personal sacrifice.

On this particular day in late January, Derek opened his office door, hung his lab coat on a metal coat rack, and sat down at his desk. He called up the latest test results on his computer.

His assistant Greg Hunt, whom Derek thought of as an earnest, albeit annoying individual, took his open door as an invitation and entered without knocking. He pulled up a chair and sat reading the results over Derek's shoulder.

"They don't look good, do they?" Greg

offered.

Derek kept his feelings of annoyance to himself. The kid obviously had a profound grasp of the obvious, but he was also a reliable worker and naive enough to have bought into Avery's story of conducting research for the betterment of humanity. This fact alone kept Derek from firing him.

"Do you think we'll continue to get funding for this experiment with no results to show?" Greg asked.

"Let me worry about the funding, Greg. I'm sure my backers are willing to be patient. We'll just have to line up some more test subjects. I'm sending you out to the campus this afternoon to drum up more recruits."

3

I was in my first year of university when they recruited me. I was studying civil engineering, reasoning that at least buildings and bridges would not talk back to me. So far, I was the same invisible person in university that I'd been in high school, although at this point in my life the urge to fit in seemed more urgent, as if university gave me a new chance at life.

I was sitting by myself in the university cafeteria, trying my best to eat an egg salad sandwich that was obviously past its best-by date, when a man in his late twenties, dressed in jeans and a t-shirt with a symbol I could not identify, handed me a flyer. He was passing them out to the occupants of each table so I took one out of politeness. I then gathered up my textbooks and headed for my last class of the day, tucking the paper into one of my books and forgetting about it as I made my way to the engineering building.

Later that evening when I was in my cubbyhole of an apartment, the paper fell out of the book, and I happened to glance at it. It read a bit like a marine recruitment poster.

> Are you your own person? Are
> you capable of thinking outside
> the box? Do you often feel
> like an outsider because you
> recognize that you are gifted?

This was followed by additional verbiage and an invitation to a meeting on campus the following Monday.

At that time I had no intention of going.

4

Derek looked up expectantly as Greg entered his office and plopped down in the visitor's chair.

"So, how'd it go with the flyers?"

"I gave out about fifty of them. Probably about half of them will end up in recycle bins, which means we'll have about twenty to thirty potential subjects to screen. Is it the same protocol this time?"

"Yes. We'll weed out those who have close family ties or are in a relationship. And anyone living in university residence. The last thing we need is meddlesome relatives or university authorities wondering why someone's missing from their dorm when we do the extended experiments."

"We don't usually have much to worry about as far as that's concerned. Judging from our past subjects, these people are usually loners who live off-campus."

Derek nodded. "Most of them—if not all—are accustomed to hiding their talents to avoid ridicule. That's why it's so important to reassure them they're accepted by their peers in the experimental group. Otherwise, we can't gauge the extent of their powers."

"What about the previous group who've shown no results? Can we have them sign a non-disclosure agreement before we give them their final stipend for the research?"

Derek scowled at him and shook his head impatiently. "You ask too many questions, Greg. All you need to know is that I've already dealt with them."

****

If Greg Hunt had a major flaw, it was perhaps that he trusted people too easily. For example, he'd missed the ominous tone of Derek's pronouncement on the previous test group, so anxious was he to continue their research. Greg was a graduate student in biology, and he'd been recruited by Derek after one of the lectures the latter had given on the potential for transhumanism to transform and improve life. Greg had waited until the room cleared and then gone up to Derek, shaking his hand and thanking him profusely for the lecture. Derek was shrewd enough to recognize his potential usefulness, and he'd hired Greg two years ago to do the everyday data entry needed for his research and to find the appropriate subjects. Compared with Derek, the young man was at the opposite end of the moral spectrum.

5

I suffer from chronic insomnia, and I ended up attending that first meeting simply because I'd had an especially lousy day. I was late for one of my classes and then nodded off and startled awake in another one, much to the amusement of the entire class. (So much for my invisibility!)

I was feeling particularly sorry for myself that evening and happened to come across the flyer, which I'd been using as a bookmark. The meeting was scheduled for 7 PM.

What the hell, I thought.

****

When I got there, about twenty other students were already present in the room. No two people sat together, and there was virtually no eye contact and no conversation, except for a few attempts at lame jokes. Everyone seemed to be nervous, as if second-guessing why they had come here.

I took a seat near the back and waited for the session to begin. I glanced up at one point and saw a woman with long blond hair and over-sized glasses—she reminded me of pictures I'd seen of a young Hillary Clinton— looking at me. She blushed and quickly looked down again.

Funny, I thought. *I can't get any type of reading from her at all.* With my empathic abilities, it was very rare that I couldn't sense something from another person.

The door to the classroom opened suddenly, and a short, nondescript man entered the room. He had thinning brown hair, and looked professorial in his horn-rimmed glasses. He approached the lectern and cleared his throat, creating unintentional feedback in the microphone. Everyone cringed. He good-naturedly made a joke about it, helping to put us at ease. I was waiting for the sales pitch and was pleasantly surprised at the man's low-key approach.

"Hello, thanks everyone for coming. My name is Dr. Derek Avery. Please call me Derek." He then proceeded to establish his credentials both as a researcher and an academic, explaining that he had a close affiliation with the international genome project currently mapping the make-up of human DNA.

It was only much later that I would learn Avery had fabricated his credentials and, by that time, it was too late.

The first session was a meet-and-greet as we stumbled over introductions and self-consciously told about ourselves. It was a transparent process, but still it worked: I started feeling a slight bond with the other people in the room, something which I'd never before experienced.

6

Derek Avery called Greg into his office to give him an update on the previous evening. "It went well. There was the usual nervousness, but they relaxed a bit as the evening progressed."

"I know it's early, but did any of them look promising?"

"Could be. They run the full gamut of abilities. There were at least two empaths and even a student who claimed to have the power of remote viewing. You don't hear of that too often." He handed his research assistant a list of names. "Do your usual due diligence in checking them out."

Greg took the list, skimming over the

names as he headed for his computer. He would begin by searching Facebook and other social media sites to eliminate those with a circle of friends and family. Derek had explained to him that this protocol was necessary to avoid outside distractions for the subjects they chose and also to minimize the possibility that details of their proprietary research might leak out. In the end, those with the smallest electronic footprint would be chosen.

7

Like Jack, Annie Somers was an empath. She'd learned of her abilities in her early childhood years. When her parents died in a car crash, she was raised by an aunt, her mother's older sister. Aunt Mary was a latter-day Victorian who still placed antimacassars on her chairs and forbade Annie from playing or even sitting in the living room. She was also very fond of the adage that children should be seen and not heard. Therefore, when Annie began to experience overwhelming emotions in the presence of others, Aunt Mary was the last person in whom she wanted to confide. Like Jack, Annie gradually learned to control the constant bombardment of emotions, but it nevertheless took a heavy toll on her. She kept to herself, seldom going outside except to attend school and her weekend job at a laundromat.

Annie left the classroom that evening feeling both apprehensive and excited. She found herself drawn to Jack mainly because she couldn't get any type of reading from him. When she discovered from his introduction that he was a fellow empath, she understood why. Like her, he had obviously built up certain barriers to protect his own thoughts and emotions.

She instinctively understood why he had chosen engineering for his major. Something empirical involving spatial, not human relations.

She herself was majoring in chemistry—the symbols of the periodic table were rigid and unchanging, unlike human emotions.

8

The second meeting began with Derek entering and writing the symbol H+ on the whiteboard. "Can anyone tell me what this stands for?"

I recognized the symbol now as being the same one on the t-shirt of the man who had distributed the flyers in the university cafeteria.

An awkward silence followed with none of us wanting to speak up, and then he continued.

"This is the international symbol for transhumanism. It has various disciplines and beliefs, but its primary objective is to make use of emerging technologies to transform the horizons of human beings. Imagine eradicating disease, prolonging human life, ending drought and starvation, even going beyond current gender distinctions. And the centre of all this is the human brain and its untapped potential. That's where all of you fit in. With your special abilities, you could lead the way for scientists to learn how to harness as yet uncharted realms of consciousness."

So much for the low-key approach, I thought.

"But what about the ethics of all this?" someone asked. "Wasn't Hitler trying to accomplish the same thing with his eugenics and the creation of a master race?"

Derek cringed at the word eugenics. "There's no comparison. The Nazis wanted to develop a superior race by the elimination of anyone they considered to be inferior. But transhumanism is a democratic movement that looks at the whole of humanity and asks how we can eliminate suffering and poverty and prolong human life. The goal is one day to control our own evolution."

Another student spoke up. "But what guarantee is there that technology will be used for the good of all humanity? No one gives away technology freely. There's always a price tag attached to it."

How astute, Derek thought. To the students he said, "Transhumanism involves the ethical treatment of technology. If you can eliminate the vagaries of disease and poverty, you empower third world countries to improve the living conditions of their people. Richer countries will automatically share technology if only out of enlightened self-interest. Fewer wars and the elimination of foreign aid are examples of the benefits of transhumanism for richer nations."

I thought his arguments were as full of holes as a colander, but I remained silent. After class, I caught up with Annie Somers and asked if she would like to join me for coffee. I wanted to see what her reaction had been to Derek Avery's speech.

I expected that she'd come up with an excuse, but to my surprise, Annie readily agreed to the invitation.

After we were seated at a cafeteria table with our drinks, I asked her what she thought of his speech.

"To be honest, I don't know what to think. There's so much controversy about transhumanism. I've read a bit about it. At the same time, if he's being genuine about his goals, I think it's worth a listen. It would be nice, for once, to think that I could contribute something instead of hiding in a corner to avoid detection."

We talked for an hour, and I realized that she too had developed a sardonic and self-deprecating sense of humour as a defence mechanism.

I thought of a game I'd made up as a kid. I called it "What's the Worst That Could Happen?" It was my way of anticipating any potential disaster and ensuring that I was always one step ahead.

Annie smiled shyly at me. "You look lost in thought."

I returned her smile. "I was just thinking that I'd like to stick around for a few more meetings to see where Avery—sorry, I guess we're supposed to call him Derek—goes with this transhumanism angle. I mean, what's the worst that could happen?"

9

Several more meetings followed. The number of attendees continued to dwindle. Later I would learn that those who had close family affiliations and therefore would be missed had been culled from the group. The remaining members had either lost both of their parents or were estranged from them and had no partner or close friends who would notice their absence.

At the end, there were only six of us remaining: four males and two females. Each of us had special psychic abilities which Derek had already tested at length. By that time, we had more or less grown familiar with each other's background.

Adele Thompson and Jonathan Stewart were telepaths capable of reading other people's thoughts. For both of them, this power had its novelty at the beginning, but the novelty quickly wore off as they realized it was not always very pleasant knowing what other people were thinking.

Adele discovered, in her early readings before she'd learned to shut out the barrage of thoughts from others, that her father was having an affair and that her mother wanted to end the marriage. More sadly, she discovered that both of them regarded her as a burden who stood in the way of their new lives.

Jonathan experienced similar unpleasant discoveries. He learned that his father was an embezzler and that his mother had a gambling addiction. He also discovered that his parents, literally, seldom gave him a second thought.

Eric Chandler was a restless youth who, as a child, had been misdiagnosed with attention deficit disorder and placed on drugs. No one understood that his restlessness stemmed from the fact that, unlike everyone else, he did not live in the here and now. Eric was a remote viewer who, in his mind, could travel huge distances and see beyond the scope of his circumscribed environment. Unfortunately, his parents were also distant: they were physically there, but had little emotional attachment to him.

Of the six people chosen for the experiment, Ben Jones had perhaps the closest to a happy home life, at least until he was twelve and his parents divorced. Then he was shunted between their two homes and fought over for his affection—each of his parents vying to be the higher bidder. As a result, Ben became wary of displaying any type of emotion. What was his gift? Ben was a psychokinetic capable of manipulating objects with his mind.

10

Annie and I had grown to be close friends. We went for coffee after each meeting, and then I walked her back to her apartment. She lived in a typical student slum apartment building: poorly constructed, noisy, and grubby with cigarette butts and beer bottles littering the front lawn.

"I'm always embarrassed by this place," she said as we approached her building, "but it's near the university and I can just barely afford the ridiculous rent the landlord is extorting from me."

I smiled to ease her discomfort. "Mine's even worse. I can watch the cockroaches carrying off my plates at night."

"Oh, lord," she exclaimed.

"Well, maybe I'm exaggerating a bit, but

it's no palace, believe me."

She hesitated and then asked suddenly, "Would you like to come in?"

I smiled and nodded. She led me to a second-floor apartment which turned out to be much larger than my own. The living room and kitchen were all one room with the appliances and a small counter and stools at one end, and some meagre furniture at the other, but she'd obviously made an effort to fix up the apartment. The paint looked new, and there was a bookcase with a small TV and PlayStation console, several hanging green plants, brightly-coloured movie and travel posters, and a futon/couch covered with a beautiful embroidered shawl.

She saw me looking at the shawl. "Everything in this room is from Value Village except that. It's my one extravagance. I bought it at a small shop on Bank Street."

She went to the tiny kitchen and began to fumble around in the cupboards. "I don't have any wine glasses, but I do have a bottle of wine here somewhere. LCBO special: I'm not even sure it has a name," she laughed self-consciously. "Would you like some? It's red. I hope that's okay. And I think I have some cheese and crackers."

There was something so tentative—so vulnerable—in her voice that without thinking I went to her and, turning her around, held her in my arms. I could feel her body relax against mine.

Then she tensed as she looked up at me and said quietly, "I'm not good at this, Jack."

"It's okay, Annie. I'm not either. We'll wing it," I said before I kissed her.

We made love in her small bedroom, and I stroked her shoulders gently afterward as she relaxed in my arms.

"It's raining out," she whispered softly. "When I was little, I loved to watch the rain. It was as if the sky were crying while the earth gently absorbed its tears."

I kissed her again, and for the first time in my life, I knew what it was like to experience emotion for myself rather than secondhand.

11

Annie lay awake listening to the comforting sound of the rain. Jack had talked to her about his chronic insomnia, but he'd finally fallen asleep just before dawn.

She watched him now as he slept. His feet stuck out from the covers because of his height, and his straight brown hair had fallen into his eyes. He looked so vulnerable. He tried to present such a brave front but, reading between the lines, she knew that Jack had suffered greatly from a total absence of parental love when he was growing up. In some ways, she'd had an easier time of it. After all, she'd had parents who loved her. After their death, she had reached an unspoken truce with her aunt: she would be given a roof over her head and three meals a day, but she should not expect any type of emotional investment while she was living in her aunt's house.

Jack stirred and then his breathing assumed the rhythm of sleep. He was such a gentle and attentive lover. This was a new experience for her after the occasional one-night stand in which she'd been merely a conduit for her partner's gratification, and had understood she'd never see the person again.

An unfamiliar calm settled over her.

So this is how it feels to be at peace.

12

After that evening, Annie and I were virtually inseparable. I think we both marvelled at how easily and completely we were able to satisfy each other's physical and emotional needs.

We decided, however, not to mention our relationship to anyone else in the group and were always careful to make separate entrances to the meetings. I'm not sure what exactly we were worried about. Perhaps we thought the other members of the group would treat us less seriously. But more likely, Annie and I felt guilty because we both superstitiously believed that we had no right to happiness and kept waiting for fate to intervene and the other shoe to drop.

13

Annie and I were both fully committed to Derek's research project by this stage. At first, we'd found it difficult to exercise our powers after spending most of our lives trying to suppress them. Gradually, however, we were beginning to let go of the feeling of shame that we'd previously associated with their use.

For his part, Derek always appeared on the surface to be patient and full of encouragement for the six members of our group. He nurtured our talents, and sometimes the classroom reminded me of an exotic circus with Ben utilizing his power of psychokinesis to dislodge objects while Eric used remote viewing to describe to us what was going on outside the building. Jonathan and Adele practised their telepathy, describing to the rest of us in great and sometimes humorous detail the thoughts of people who passed by in the corridor. Annie and I contributed by describing the emotions of those people we had encountered that day in our classes. There was a strict rule that we would not attempt to practise our talents on other members of the group to avoid making anyone feel uncomfortable. But the rest of the campus was fair game to us.

After more than three months spent in meetings, Derek suddenly announced one day that during the upcoming spring break, he'd be arranging for a shuttle to take us to a private location where we could hone our skills for the final phase of testing.

****

When Derek finally sent for the six of us, we were ready. Each of us had been told to pack a suitcase and be prepared to attend a final information and experimentation session that would probably last about two weeks. He made it sound like an exotic vacation and in truth all of us were looking forward to it. Because it was the spring break at university, none of us was anxious to be the only one left behind as the other students went home to their families and friends. And we had been promised a generous remuneration for our time. With student loans to repay, we could all use a bit of extra spending money.

The van came in the early evening and by the time I boarded it, the other five members of the group had already been picked up. It felt a bit like we were going to camp, I thought, although none of us had done so when we were young, and there was joking and camaraderie among us.

The mood became a bit more sombre as the van left the university behind and travelled outside the city. When I inquired about our exact destination, the driver was deliberately vague, telling me only that we'd be there soon. He switched on the radio to avoid any further conversation. I glanced at Annie and saw that she could also sense a nervousness in the driver that neither of us could explain. Was he worried about the snow in the forecast? Was he anxious to get to his destination and return home? Or was there another explanation?

14

The journey from Ottawa took almost three hours. Eric, who was 6'5" and whose legs had been cramped during the trip, was the first one out of the van. He pulled up short, blocking the rest of us. "What the hell, is this someone's idea of a joke? Because if it is, it's a really bad one." He finally moved aside so we could leave the van.

I was the second one out of the vehicle, and I stared with dismay at the building before me, which looked like an abandoned institution. It was a massive, decrepit structure with crumbling limestone. The smell of rot was prevalent, and I was suddenly overwhelmed with a sense of misery and despair. It was as if the building should bear a sign saying: "Abandon hope all ye who enter here."

The other four members of our group joined Eric and me, staring forlornly at the building and silently shaking their heads. I glanced instinctively at Annie and saw her stricken look.

As if on cue, Derek Avery emerged from the massive iron door at the front of the building and walked tentatively down the decaying concrete steps. "I know, I know, it looks revolting from the outside, but it's a heritage building and a work in progress. Once you come inside, you'll see that you'll be quite comfortable in here with the renovations that have been made." He instructed the van driver to unload our suitcases, and made small talk as he herded us inside.

****

For his part, the driver was only too glad to be out of there. Although he was being well-paid for his shuttle service, he was always unnerved by the sight of the decrepit building. And he didn't want to think about what might be going on inside it.

15

Derek led us into a large room that looked as if it had at one time been a cafeteria. The walls had been freshly painted, and there was a large circular table in the centre surrounded by chairs. Off to one side was a banquet table covered with serving warmers holding various metal dishes, an assortment of fruits and salads, and a large urn of coffee.

"This was once a beautiful structure, but as you can see from the outside, it's fallen into a state of disrepair," Derek explained as he beckoned us to the wooden table and watched as we were seated. "The restoration funds are gradually trickling in, and the place is being renovated bit by bit. We're actually on a 950-acre stretch of mostly farmland with a nearby river. There's even a small island close to us."

"What was this place originally?" I asked.

Derek averted his eyes and mumbled something inaudible.

"I'm sorry, I didn't hear you," Annie said.

"I'm always a bit hesitant to discuss the building's origins in case it puts people off," Derek explained, "but it was originally a hospital for the insane and later a sanitarium for patients with tuberculosis. The building has a storied history," he added, "and will be magnificent once it's been completely renovated— But your supper is getting cold. Let's move to the buffet table. I'm sure you'll enjoy the food here. Just one of your many perks."

I can't see how this dreadful building would offer any perks, I thought. *It's cold and forsaken ... and isolated.*

The six members of our group, along with Derek, served ourselves at the buffet table. Despite our misgivings about the place, we were hungry, and there was little conversation as we ate. When we had finished, Derek introduced us to his assistant, Greg Hunt, who was to finish the session with us by discussing the various details of our stay. I recognized him as the person who had distributed the flyers in the university cafeteria. He was rail-thin with a mop of unruly blond hair and for some reason he reminded me of an overly-eager Labrador retriever puppy.

"Hi, welcome to your new temporary home, be it ever so humble."

No one laughed at Greg's feeble attempt at humour.

He continued. "Derek has deliberately chosen this building because of its location. We're far enough away from the city to avoid distractions so there will be no 'corruption' of the trial results from outside stimuli. For that reason there's no cellphone reception or internet connectivity here. But I don't think you'll miss them because you'll be too busy with the experimental trials, and if you do get fidgety, we have a small library of mysteries and thrillers, and there are several acres that you can explore as long as you let me know beforehand that you're leaving the building.

"As Derek has indicated, I'm his assistant, and I'll be working closely with each of you. I have a graduate degree in biology, and I've worked with him for two years now, helping him with his research. You'll probably get sick of seeing me after a while."

Again the attempt at humour fell flat.

"Do you have any questions before I show you your rooms? They're small but comfortable. I have one myself."

Eric spoke up. "I don't see why you feel the need to cut us off from civilization like this. Surely, the trials could have been conducted somewhere else with minimal intrusion. I mean, no internet or cellphones—"

The rest of us also indicated our displeasure with the living arrangements.

Greg seemed very uncomfortable with this dissent. "I don't make the rules here. If you have concerns, please feel free to take them up with Derek in the morning. In the meantime, I'll show you your rooms."

****

As I entered my room, I saw that it was small, but serviceable. The walls had been painted blue, perhaps for the calming effect of the colour. There was a twin bed and bedside stand, a closet, and a bathroom with a shower stall in the corner of the room.

I noticed, however, that the weak ceiling light did little to dispel the darkness. Looking for a window, I saw one recessed at the top of the wall opposite the bed. The ceilings were so high that it was not within reach. I noted with growing alarm that it was barred.

Greg saw me glance toward the window and anticipated my question. "The bars are a quaint touch, aren't they? They were preserved from the original structure. The architect wanted to ensure that the historical integrity of the building was respected, so I've been told. Don't worry about them, I have them in my room as well."

16

Later that evening, Greg spoke to Derek on his cellphone. Derek had insisted he lie to the group and tell them there was no wireless connectivity.

"So, how did it go, Greg?" Derek inquired.

"About what you would expect. Lots of complaints about not having access to their cellphones and the internet. And they were all alarmed by the bars on the bedroom windows."

"Did they buy your story about 'historical integrity'?"

"They don't really have a choice, do they?"

"Well, they're stuck there for the time being, and they know if they balk too much they won't get the money I promised them.

And, more importantly," Derek added, "they won't be able to test their powers in the trials, and I've made very sure to dangle that carrot before them. It's become a part of their identity, seeing as they're all social misfits.

"Anyway, Greg, thanks. I'll see you first thing in the morning. Hunnicutt and his crew will be outside as usual to make sure everyone stays tucked in their comfy beds."

"Do you really think that's necessary? The guards make me nervous. Besides, where's anyone going to go in this godforsaken place?"

"I told you before, Greg, that we need to ensure everyone's safety, as well as their cooperation."

"I just find this an odd way to operate, is all, Derek. I'm surprised that your government backers would support this type of security."

My backers *would take you out in a second, Greg, if they thought you were asking too many questions*, Derek thought. But to his assistant he said simply, "It's okay, Greg. Don't worry. I have everything under control."

17

I awoke during the night and forgot for a moment where I was. The room was pitch black. I automatically looked for a clock radio on the bedside stand, but there was none. Then I remembered last evening's journey. I groped for the lamp beside my bed and finally found the switch.

I searched the table for my watch which I distinctly remembered taking off before I went to bed. But it was nowhere to be found.

My sense of unease grew as I felt the coldness in the room. I knew instinctively that the new bedrooms had been constructed in the old sleeping quarters of the asylum. The drywall that had probably been put up hastily did nothing to dampen the chill. It seemed makeshift, and its blue paint could not disguise the underlying reality of the misery of those who had been incarcerated in this institution. I shivered as I felt the cold in my bones, and in my mind I thought I heard the ghost voices of all those who had lived and died here without hope.

I glanced up at the barred window, as if seeking some way to escape this misery, and could see disembodied lights. Lanterns? Flashlights? Was someone making the rounds of the building?

I'm glad we're only going to be here for two weeks. I hope Annie will be okay.

****

Annie hadn't been able to talk to Jack alone either at the group's late dinner or afterward when Greg Hunt had quickly ushered them to their individual rooms. If she didn't know better, she'd almost think that Derek and Greg were deliberately trying to keep the members of the group isolated from each other. But for what purpose?

It was after midnight—or so she assumed since there was no bedside clock and she'd forgotten to bring her watch—but she hadn't managed to fall asleep yet.

She'd sensed a barrier when she tried to read the emotions of Derek and Greg, as if they were blocking her, but at one point Greg had let down his guard, and she could feel his uneasiness.

What is it they're not telling us?

A sense of misery came over her: so profound that it almost paralysed her.

There are hundreds of unheard voices trapped in the walls of this asylum. So many stories that will forever remain untold.

****

In their respective rooms, Jonathan and Adele were also feeling intense discomfort. Try as they might, neither had been able to penetrate the minds of Avery and Hunt. There was some sort of ... barrier.

Adele, are you still awake? Jonathan directed his thoughts toward her. *Is this place weird or what? What have the six of us gotten ourselves into?*

Lying awake, Adele sensed Jonathan's thoughts and replied mentally. *I'm frightened, Jonathan. Something's not right with Derek Avery bringing us to this place. Why here, surrounded by the ghosts of the helpless who had no one to honour them in life or mourn their passing? I can't get their voices out of my head!*

****

In his room Eric was also lying sleepless. He too saw the lights outside. He used his power of remote viewing to survey the exterior grounds of the building, and then wished he hadn't.

There were six men dressed in khaki guard uniforms patrolling the perimeter of the building.

What disturbed him most was not their presence, but the revolvers holstered in their belts.

****

Ben was the only one of the six who had fallen into a deep sleep. He tossed and turned in his bed in the throes of a nightmare in which the mouldering limestone bricks of the building were falling apart one by one and trapping him beneath their weight.

He was trying to use his power of psychokinesis to remove the bricks, but the weight was overwhelming him.

****

The six members of the group would have been even more alarmed if by chance they had tried to open their bedroom doors.

They were all locked.

18

Derek Avery arrived before 7 AM the next morning and let himself into the building. He also quietly unlocked each of the bedroom doors through a remote control device.

Greg was up and making coffee, so Derek joined him. "Good morning, how did they do last night?"

"I haven't had a chance to review all of the camera feed from their rooms, but it looked like they were fairly restless, which is to be expected the first night in strange surroundings. I don't think putting them in this asylum helps. Funny that such an incredibly huge building could be so claustrophobic: as if everywhere you go, the walls are closing in on you."

"You're not turning Gothic on me, are

you, Greg? That's all I need. Next you'll be telling me the place is haunted! Tonight we'll simply start dosing their food to make them sleepy and more compliant. The drug helped with the last group."

Greg protested, "It took the edge off them, but they were still ready to revolt after two weeks. How long do you plan to keep this group here?"

"As long as it takes to see results," Derek replied. "Now let's set up the stuff I brought from the caterer for their breakfast."

"I still don't see why we can't have a cook here. It would make it a lot simpler."

"You know the answer to that, Greg. The fewer people that know about this place, the better. I'm already paying a fortune to keep the construction crew away. Not to mention the cost of the guards.

"By the way, Hunnicutt reported an incident from last night. He said several of the bricks from the east wall came loose all of a sudden and tumbled on the walkway. And he said that part of the building had already been inspected and was supposed to be structurally sound."

19

I awoke the next morning feeling tired and disoriented. I had no idea what time it was. I still hadn't found my watch. I showered and shaved and then went to the dining room in search of breakfast. The other five members of our group were already eating so I helped myself at the buffet table and joined them. I noticed that Derek was sitting with the others and seemed to be monopolizing the conversation.

"Good morning, Jack. I hope you slept well." Derek didn't give me time to reply before he continued. "I was just outlining the day's schedule with the rest of the group. You're going to be very busy from now on. Starting tomorrow, we'll move breakfast up to 7 AM. Then each of you will go to your assigned laboratory room where we'll continue evaluating and sharpening your abilities. A quick lunch at noon, and then it's back to your labs for more testing."

"Sounds like a heavy schedule," Annie commented, "but I guess we'll have few distractions here. I notice, by the way, that there are no clocks or calendars in this building. Is that intentional?"

"Smart girl," Derek said patronizingly. "You're right: it's part of the protocol for your clinical trials. I want you focusing solely on the lab experiments, not worrying about when it's time for supper or when you'll be returning to the university. For the moment, think of it as having all the time in the world."

Maybe they took my watch, I thought. But some instinct of self-preservation made me decide not to mention its disappearance. *I don't want to make waves right now. I'll wait to see what the day brings.*

The clinical trials began in earnest after our breakfast, and were much more strenuous than anything to date we had been tested on at the university. The lab rooms were painted white and were devoid of both windows and furnishings other than two wooden chairs placed facing each other with a portable cloth divider between the two, and a table that held recording devices and a DVD player. There were video cameras mounted on the wall facing the chairs. Greg and Derek circulated among the rooms, giving each member of the group his or her instructions.

In my respective lab room, I was given pads of paper and instructed to listen to a series of audio recordings. I was told to jot down my impressions of the emotions underlying the dialogue of each of the speakers. It was a difficult task because the voices were neutral in tone. It required deep concentration and after the first tape and the subsequent debriefing, I noticed that I'd lost all track of time. I thought of Annie and wondered if she was undergoing a similar battery of tests.

I learned later that Jonathan and Adele also underwent strenuous testing. Each was required to decipher and record the thoughts of a series of people whose images were projected on the blank walls of their lab rooms. At second remove, without actually having the individuals nearby, they were finding it difficult, if not impossible, to complete the task.

According to his later account, Ben was the only one that day who'd had any success. He was able to move most of the objects that they'd placed on a table behind a screen.

Of all of us, his extrasensory power had developed the most during the months we'd spent with Derek.

****

I noted the same pattern at lunchtime as at breakfast: although we would sit together, we were largely unable to communicate among ourselves because Derek was always talking.

I decided to try an experiment of my own. I projected my thoughts toward Jonathan and Adele. *Derek obviously doesn't want us talking to one another. He and Greg have managed, for the most part, to mask their emotions—I'm not sure how. Are you able to pick up any stray thoughts from them? If you hear me, please don't nod or give any indication. I'm going to get up from the table shortly to pour another cup of coffee. Can one of you follow in a minute and just shake your head or nod to indicate whether you're picking up thoughts from the two of them?*

I'd been listening to Derek talk about the importance of his work while I was trying to exchange thoughts with Jonathan and Adele. I made desultory small talk and after a few moments rose and said, "I'm going to get a refill on my coffee. I need an extra caffeine boost for this afternoon's session."

A few moments passed and then Jonathan said, "I think Jack's got the right idea. I could use some extra caffeine as well." He pushed away from the table and joined me at the buffet. When I glanced up at him, Jonathan shook his head almost imperceptibly.

20

After lunch, Derek summoned Greg to join him in his makeshift office in the building. "Close the door, Greg. I don't want to take the chance of being overheard."

"What's up?"

"This group has much stronger abilities than the last one. That's excellent from one perspective: if I can sell my clients on their potential usefulness, I'll finally be getting somewhere. But it's also worrisome because I can sense some of them trying hard to probe my thoughts and emotions. We're going to have to ensure that our mental barriers remain in place. For now, the self-hypnosis is working for both of us, and we can keep them at bay. But we'll have to take other measures if our defences start to slip."

Greg nodded, but said nothing. His usual unflagging optimism was starting to fail him because he hated this place, and for once he caught the note of menace in Derek's voice.

21

It was her second night there, and Annie still hadn't had an opportunity to talk to Jack about the place. She'd seen him only in passing in the hallway outside the lab rooms, and at meals Derek made it next to impossible for them to speak openly among themselves.

She was exhausted from the day's testing sessions, which had not gone well for her. Her eyes felt heavy-lidded, and she fell asleep fully-clothed on her bed.

****

Jonathan and Adele were communicating telepathically between their two rooms. But both of them felt inexplicably languid as if their thoughts were muddled this evening. They said good night mentally and soon were both asleep.

****

Eric was once again distantly viewing the grounds of the building. The guards had not yet appeared. At first he saw only field after field of overgrown farmland, but then his vision focused on a decrepit stone fountain consisting of three intricate carved bowls supported by statues of cherubs.

It must have been lovely when it was working—its beauty so incongruous in this place of misery.

He continued to view his surroundings: in addition to the overgrown acres, he glimpsed several abandoned buildings that perhaps had once housed farm and maintenance equipment, and his mind was lulled by the sight of water lapping placidly on the far shore.

Just before he fell asleep, his mind saw but did not register a cemetery showing signs of freshly-dug graves.

****

Ben was asleep in his room and once again he was dreaming. He was examining the west side of the structure when suddenly the cupola on the roof, housing a huge weather vane shaped like a galloping horse, collapsed. In his nightmare he was impaled by one of the arrows of the weather vane when it crashed to the ground.

22

"How did they sleep last night? Any better?" Derek inquired of Greg as he joined him the next morning.

"They all fell asleep early so the medication is obviously working. Let's just hope it doesn't dull their performance today."

"It's an experimental drug that's not known to have any side effects of that nature, but it will take their bodies a while to adjust to the medication. They may be a bit off for a couple of days like the previous group was.

"By the way, can you give that caretaker I hired a call and see if he can clear up some debris? There must have been a strong wind last night. That weather vane came down off the roof. Good job there was no one standing underneath it. That thing must weigh at least two hundred pounds. God knows how they got it up there in the first place."

23

The second day went much as the first had with morning and afternoon rounds of testing broken only by meals. At lunchtime Annie and I managed to exchange quick hellos at the buffet.

"Feeling any better about being here?" I asked.

"Not really, but I guess I can stand it for two weeks. Beyond that I'd be climbing the walls."

"How's the testing going for you? I'm finding it very difficult."

"Me too," Annie said as she offered me the first genuine smile I'd seen since we'd arrived here. "I guess I was getting too complacent about my abilities. This is a whole new level for me. It's especially hard when it's disembodied voices and you can't even see the person. Oh well. I'll keep trying to improve as I go along." She touched me gently on the arm before returning to the table.

I glanced over as Annie seated herself. I couldn't help but notice that Derek was glaring at her.

It's not my imagination then. He definitely doesn't want us talking to each other.

****

After supper that night, Greg announced he would be taking us on a walk. "I know it must be difficult for you to be cooped up here. Grab your jackets, and let's have a look around the property. I think you'll be pleasantly surprised."

He led us outside. "Stay together please. Believe it or not, it's pretty easy to get lost around here. And there's debris from the building, not to mention about a million groundhog holes to avoid."

Greg directed our group toward a grassy area that looked as if it had recently been cleared. There was a fire pit in the centre and several wooden benches. "It's still chilly, but this will eventually be a wonderful place to sit. The caretaker will be planting flowers when it's time, and it should be quite pleasant here in the summer."

"I'm sure the flowers will be lovely in bloom," Annie said, "but we'll be long gone by then."

For a second I could sense that Greg's barrier had slipped.

There was that nervousness again.

He recovered quickly, however, and started showing us other points of interest. "I don't know if you can make it out on the horizon, but that's the island that once formed part of the estate. I'm told the patients were taken on boat trips there as part of their recovery process. Then the government sold the land to rich cottagers from the city. The excursions stopped because the new owners didn't want the patients coming over for 'safety' reasons. There had at one time been a plan to build a bridge across from this side, but that fell through because of the cottagers' complaints. There's a bridge on the far side of the island to connect to the mainland."

"Are there any people living on the island, now?" I inquired.

Greg looked at me sharply. "I haven't been over there. I guess any cottages that used to be there have long since rotted."

24

A week had passed. Although I frequently lost track of time, I was monitoring the days by the number of experimentation sessions. Derek had advised us that he was happy with our progress to date and said he would be increasing the difficulty of the tests in the following weeks.

"You said 'weeks' plural. We just have one week left here and then spring break will be over and we'll need to get back to university," I said.

"Sorry, just a slip of the tongue. I meant over the course of the next week," Derek replied.

But the other members of our group looked worried as if they didn't believe him either.

Ben spoke up. "You're going to make

sure that our return shuttle is ready at the end of next week to take us back, aren't you? I mean, I think I speak for the others that we're all grateful for the opportunity you've given us to develop our abilities without negative consequences. But at the same time we have academic commitments."

The rest of us nodded anxiously.

"You guys worry too much about little things. Of course you'll be going home next weekend. I might even let you leave on Saturday to give you a day to rest up before you resume your classes. And of course we'll continue to meet on a regular basis on the campus to move ahead with our tests."

He's lying, I thought, although Derek himself maintained a bland expression, giving nothing away.

25

The intensity of the experimentation increased dramatically the second week. Derek used various forms of sensory deprivation, including blindfolding, to make the tests more difficult. In addition, he introduced rock music and soundtracks filled with loud noises to see if the group could focus on their tasks. The results were mixed at first, but by the end of the second week, he was pleased with their progress.

"As I said before, they're much stronger than the first group," he remarked to Greg at one of their early morning meetings.

"They're getting restless to go back to university, Derek. When do you plan to tell them they'll be here another two weeks?"

"I'll tell them at supper tonight."

"They won't be pleased!"

"Don't worry, Greg. I'll finesse the news."

Greg looked doubtful but said nothing.

****

At supper Derek announced that he had some good news to share with us. We all looked up expectantly from our plates. "I've made arrangements with your professors so you can stay an additional two weeks without any fear of getting behind in your studies. In light of the importance of this experiment, they're willing to provide tutors to catch you up quickly on your work. I said I'd pay for their services, of course."

"This is *good* news?" Annie asked dejectedly. "We were looking forward to going back. Why can't you just continue the testing at the university like you were doing before?"

Derek replied condescendingly, "My dear, you must realize how much progress you're making. I simply don't have the facilities at the university for testing that I have here."

I spoke up in Annie's defence. "There's no need to be patronizing. Annie said what we're all thinking. We planned to leave tomorrow and as far as I'm concerned, we're going tomorrow unless, of course, anyone actually wants to stay here for another two weeks?" I looked around at the other group members, who were shaking their heads vigorously. "Then it's settled and we go back tomorrow. You'll just have to make other arrangements for testing at the university."

****

The next morning, the six of us brought our packed suitcases with us and stowed them in the corner of the dining room in anticipation of leaving.

There was no sign of Derek, but Greg greeted us at the dining room table as if it were a normal day. "Good morning. Everyone sleep well? Ready for another busy day?"

I pointed to our suitcases in the corner. "I think you've forgotten that we leave today."

Greg feigned ignorance. "But didn't Derek tell you he made arrangements for you to stay another two weeks?"

"He did, but we all respectfully declined his hospitality," I said, not bothering to hide my sarcasm.

"Well, I'm afraid you don't really have a choice. The shuttle bus is our only means of transportation, and it's not coming back for two weeks. In fact, the driver booked vacation once he heard you were staying longer."

There was dead silence at the table.

This isn't right. Now, I really feel like a prisoner here, I thought, as a sense of panic rose in me. And I didn't need to be an empath to read the looks of the others.

I had just been outwitted at my own game of what's the worst that could happen.

26

Derek had left Greg in charge of the group and was meeting with his clients in Ottawa. There were currently two American companies offering military and security services who were funding his research with the understanding that his product would be sold to the higher bidder. He was currently meeting with representatives of one of these companies.

After shaking hands and exchanging pleasantries, the three men settled in at the conference table in the room Derek had rented for the meeting.

"Gentlemen, I'm pleased to say that the second round of testing has commenced, and I'm very impressed with the group we've selected. They're undergoing rigorous evaluation right now at a secure location."

One of the representatives spoke up. "I'm afraid I wasn't in attendance at the last meeting. Can you tell me how your experiment is relevant to our military and security operations?"

Derek explained, "The United States already has machines—drones—that can target and kill its enemies at a great distance. Imagine, then, what you could achieve if you had personnel who could view terrorist cells from a remote location, read their thoughts and emotions, and manipulate objects within their camps to create chaos. Think of the capacity for gaining intelligence in order to identify potential plots and thwart them, the number of lives that could be saved, and the ability to turn the enemies' weapons against themselves through psychokinetic manipulation."

"But what use would these personnel be if they're not trained soldiers? How would they understand what's vital intelligence, for example?"

"They would be embedded with soldiers and learn from them how to recognize the enemy. And eventually they would identify those within the military ranks with similar talents that could be developed through training."

The other representative spoke up. "I

thought the Defense Intelligence Agency tried to establish a program like that in the 1970s and decided it was a waste of time. I think the files have recently been declassified, and there was absolutely no success reported."

Derek scoffed. "I'm not talking about that ludicrous *Men Staring at Goats* stuff. That was decades ago. We know a hell of a lot more now about the human mind and how it can be manipulated."

"If that's the case, when will you be able to give us a demonstration?"

"I need at least another three months with my research subjects. Then I'll have something concrete to show you."

****

Derek sat in the conference room after the others had left and allowed himself to relish the feeling of power. He not only had control over his test subjects, but also had held sway over the representatives at this meeting.

Success is so near, I can taste it.

He thought of his parents, who had died almost penniless after putting him through university.

They were content with small potatoes, but I never was. Dad was always telling me

I needed to work hard to succeed in life. No shortcuts, he said. And where did that get him? A paltry old age pension after forty years of working in that pitiful little store.

No, dear departed Dad, you were wrong. There are shortcuts. I can succeed with minimal effort. I already make ten times more than you ever did, and I'll soon be very rich.

My philosophy is the best one: play the suckers for all they're worth.

27

Greg was getting more and more nervous. Derek had told him he'd paid off the previous test group, but something didn't seem right about his explanation. He'd seemed too defensive and dismissive of his inquiries. Greg didn't understand why. He'd tried to track down the six previous subjects to no avail. The registrar's office at the university had of course denied him any information because of privacy legislation. He'd expected no less. And his searches on social media were fruitless because they'd deliberately chosen subjects with no real family or friends.

He fingered the duplicate he'd made of Derek's office key. Greg, of course, had keys to their main office in Ottawa, but he'd had to resort to theft to get this key for Derek's asylum office. He felt guilty about copying it. After all, he'd been with him for two years.

Derek was in Ottawa now, attending a meeting with the experiment's government backers. He would not be back today, as far as Greg knew.

Pushing away from his desk, he rose and made his way to Derek's office. He desperately wanted to search the files to see if there was any clue as to what had happened to the previous team of subjects. He unlocked the door and went to the filing cabinet.

Suddenly he heard a sound outside the door. Had Derek returned early from his meeting? In his haste, as he went to investigate the source of the noise, he knocked a bunch of papers from the desk.

After listening for several seconds at the door, he realized the sound was coming from the dining room. *Probably just someone getting a snack.*

Greg went back to the office undetected and stooped to pick up the papers he'd scattered from the desk. He happened to glance at one of them and realized it was a glossy brochure from an American military outfit. The group had changed its name since their disastrous involvement in the death of civilians during the Iraq War, but he recognized the new name from newspaper accounts.

Suddenly, Greg felt sick. *Is this who Derek is meeting with today? Did he lie to me about having Canadian government backers? What else did he lie to me about?*

And then Greg had a sinking feeling that he knew what had happened to the previous test group.

And it was not good.

28

Now that we'd openly acknowledged our hostility toward staying in this decrepit building any longer, Derek and Greg were watching us even more closely and trying as best they could to keep us from communicating with each other.

I should explain that our evenings were regulated almost as tightly as our days. Once supper was over, we were usually herded to a supervised walk outside—ostensibly to give us some exercise but more probably to wear us out after an exhausting series of trials each day.

I'd begun to suspect that our food was being drugged because I was sleeping soundly after years of chronic insomnia, and I could no longer sense the overwhelming despair of unseen spirits at night. I had no way of identifying what food contained the medication. I had stopped drinking the coffee in case, ironically, that was how they were sedating us, but it hadn't made for any change in my new sleep patterns.

I'd become aware by this point that our every move was being monitored by cameras. I'd found the camera in my bedroom purely by accident when I'd noticed the lamplight glinting off a metal object embedded in the wall. I hadn't dislodged it, but I'd seen enough spy movies to figure out what it was. After this discovery, I'd managed to identify a whole series of cameras mounted throughout the building.

I knew instinctively that the additional two weeks would not be the end of it, and I wondered what more they had in store for us. Something was nagging at my consciousness, but I couldn't recall exactly what it was. Then I remembered when Greg had shown us the area of the garden on our first walk outside. Annie had commented that we wouldn't be here to see the flowers in bloom, and he'd displayed nervousness. Was it because he knew that we might still be there?

The only unsurveilled location I could find was the tiny room that served as a library with a couple of shelves of paperbacks.

There were a few Dean Koontz novels; a beat-up copy of Stephen King's *Firestarter* and some other earlier works; a collection of John Grisham novels; and a liberal sampling of Michael Connelly. Why they chose not to oversee this area with cameras, I had no idea. Perhaps they thought that if we ventured here, we'd just grab a book and leave. But for me, the lack of surveillance was fortuitous because it gave Annie and me a chance to meet in private.

I gave her a quick hug this evening and asked, "Did anyone see you come in here?" I was trying to gauge how much time we had before someone came looking for us.

"No, I don't think so. Derek's gone for the day, and I managed to slip a note to Eric asking him to waylay Greg after supper. The last I saw, the two of them were engaged in an animated discussion, and I don't think Greg saw me leave.

"Oh, Jack, I'm worried we'll never get out of here."

I'd been thinking the same thing but I tried to put on my game face for Annie's sake. "Well, it's only for two more weeks."

"No, Jack, we don't have the luxury of waiting two weeks. Two weeks will extend to four and then six..."

Our conversation was suddenly interrupted by Eric, who was making frantic arm signals to tell us someone was coming.

We started to walk back to our rooms when we were waylaid by Greg. "I'd like to see you and Annie in my office."

I felt the bile rise in my throat as Annie and I followed him down the hall.

29

When Annie and I entered Greg's office, we were prepared for the worst, expecting that he had discovered our method of communication. We sat down in front of his desk, but what he said next floored us.

"I know that the two of you are a couple—don't bother denying it because I've seen the way you look at each other when you think no one's watching— and I don't have any problem with that, but if Derek finds out, he won't be pleased. He doesn't like his research subjects growing too close. He views it as a challenge to his authority. So I'm going to help the two of you get out of here—"

"But ... why would you be willing to help us?" Annie asked. "I thought the two of you were in this together."

Greg hesitated for a moment, probably wondering how far he should go in telling us the truth. Then he seemed to make up his mind. "Because you're not the first group of subjects. And I can't find out what happened to the last group. Derek assures me they were paid their stipend and sent on their way, but it doesn't seem that they went back to university. In fact, I can't find any trace of them—"

"What the hell do you mean?" I interjected. "What could have happened to them?"

There was another long pause from Greg. "The whole group was brought to this place and their stay kept getting extended the same way yours has been. Derek was extremely upset because a couple of them threatened to report him to the police. They were going to accuse him of unlawful confinement.

"Anyway, I'm willing to help you, as much as I can. I think you and Annie should go together—a couple would have more luck flagging down help—and then send the police for the rest of your group."

"But can't you call the police yourself?" I asked incredulously. "It would be a lot easier for you to get access to a phone than us."

"I can't risk it. I'm sure Derek would find out. The best I can do is try to find you a way out of here. I've done a fair amount of exploring because I've been so restless. There's a collapsed boathouse on the property with an old rowboat inside. You can use it to get to the island. I told you no one was living there, but I lied. I've seen lights at night so I'm sure there must still be houses there or hunting camps and cottages. You'll have to get across quickly while it's dark and then see if you can get someone to help you once you're on the island. There's just one major problem—"

"What?" I asked.

"I'm going to tell Derek that we lost power because of a storm. The two of you will have to row across in a thunderstorm, which means you'll be sitting ducks if the guards spot you during flashes of lightning."

"I think I can get Ben to help out," I said. "He can use his psychokinesis to create a distraction so the guards will be drawn away from the edge of the water."

"I've checked online for the weather," Greg said, and before I could interrupt him again, he said, "Yes, I had to lie to you about that as well. There's a remote wireless connection here, and I do have a computer and cellphone that I use to contact Derek."

Both of us looked at him and shook our heads in disgust.

"Regardless of what you think of me, I'm trying to help you now. There's a storm forecast for this Thursday night. They're common this time of year. That only gives us three days to plan everything."

30

Three days ... it was so little time in which to prepare. But Annie and I were willing to take the chance to get out of here and help our friends. We didn't even want to think about what might have happened to the members of the first group.

Our first task was to send a note to Ben to help us create a distraction for the guards. Greg had implored us to ask Ben to respect the need for secrecy. His reasoning was that it would be next to impossible to get all of us away without detection. It was a more manageable plan with just Annie and me. He had an ulterior motive as well, I suspect: he didn't want to face Derek alone and have to concoct a realistic story about how he'd managed to let all of us escape.

Our main objective was to get to the police as quickly as possible to avoid any retaliation against the others. This weighed very heavily on our minds.

That night, I kept going over everything we needed to do to prepare for the escape. There was something bothering me, but I couldn't quite put my finger on it. Then, just as I was nodding off to sleep, I realized what it was. Although it had been an early spring and unseasonably warm, there were bound to be chunks of ice in the river that could destroy a small boat. Or worse still, we might encounter frozen sections that would keep us from ever making it to the island.

So many things that could go wrong. But we have no choice.

31

Finally it was Thursday evening. Annie and I were incredibly nervous and had little appetite, but forced ourselves to eat and to listen to Derek's endless small talk at supper. We knew from Greg that Derek would be leaving around 7:00 PM, but still the meal seemed interminable.

Greg had agreed to meet the two of us in the library to give us the clear signal once Derek had left. We were waiting there now. It was already 7:30 PM and still he hadn't surfaced. We were beginning to worry that the escape might need to be called off. Then Greg finally appeared and urged us in a stage whisper to come to his office. I noticed immediately that his hands were shaking uncontrollably. I could only hope that he hadn't appeared this nervous to Derek.

"I'm going to show you where the control panel is located to shut off the power. You're going to have to hurry. The guards will be here any minute. You'll need to knock me out to make this escape realistic." He handed me a heavy iron paperweight from his desk.

"Are you sure this is necessary?" I asked. I had a lot of reasons to hate this guy, but I'd never physically assaulted anyone in my life, and I didn't know how much pressure to apply.

"Yeah, I've only got a chance to convince Derek if I have a plausible story. I'm ready when you are."

I felt the bulk of the paperweight in my hand and tried to gauge how hard I needed to hit him. I didn't want to kill him, for Christ's sake. Then I swung it toward the back of his head. He slumped over his desk, and I felt his wrist to make sure there was a pulse. I breathed a heavy sigh of relief that he was still alive.

Annie hit the switch on the control panel to cut off the electrical supply to the building so the cameras and locks would be disengaged. We had to hurry: we were running half an hour late already and we needed to get to the boathouse.

****

Ben was getting more and more nervous. Something was wrong. He should have heard a knock on his door a long time ago. That was to be the signal that Jack and Annie had escaped. Then he was to wait fifteen minutes before dislodging bricks from the far side of the building to distract the guards.

The knock finally came and he recognized the urgency in it. They'd already lost precious time. He'd have to begin soon.

Concentrating with all his might, he finally managed to loosen some of the bricks. Then he rested for a moment.

Suddenly he saw the flashlight beams of the guards reflected off his bedroom window. With a final push of all of his psychokinetic energy, he saw in his mind's eye the bricks tumble to the ground.

If only I'm not too late.

****

I opened the front door cautiously. The guards were not in sight, so we ran quickly, using our flashlights to guide us to the boathouse. With dismay I saw that it would take several minutes to remove the boat from the ruins of the building. Greg hadn't been able to leave the boat outside in case it drew attention when the guards made their rounds.

The two of us heaved on it, careful to avoid the fallen beams of the structure, and finally tugged it free. But the movement caused more boards to collapse, and I was afraid the noise would alert the guards. Annie and I held our breath and waited, but thankfully there was no sound of approaching footsteps.

32

Hunnicutt, the leader of the guards, swore silently as he heard the noise from the far side of the building. *What now?* He ordered his men to check out the source of the disturbance. He planned to stay in place until they returned, but then he heard their shouts and rushed to their side.

He saw immediately that a large brick and chunk of mortar had fallen on Matthews, one of his men, who was lying motionless on the ground. He knelt down to feel his pulse. It was thready and it was obvious that Matthews was having trouble breathing. He tossed his keys to one of the others. "Bring the van around. I need to get him to a hospital. He's not doing well."

The guard grabbed the keys and headed for the front of the building. He was so distracted by his friend's condition that he failed to notice the distant sound of oars slapping the water.

Hunnicutt and his men moved Matthews into the van, supporting his head carefully. Then he gunned the engine, heading for the hospital, while the other men stood around abjectly, each thinking that he could have been the one lying near death in the van.

33

We heard the crash of the bricks and immediately started to move the boat into the water. I prayed silently that we would have enough time. The two of us jumped into the boat and started rowing. There had been no life jackets in the boat, adding to the recklessness of our attempt to escape.

We'd only been rowing for about five minutes, when we heard the echo of a shout. I thought they'd discovered our escape, and I looked in despair at Annie. But there were no further sounds and no nearby movement. It would take us about twenty minutes to reach the island.

After about fifteen minutes, our arms were aching with the frantic rowing as we maneuvered around floes of ice that would have easily destroyed the boat.

Suddenly the sky lit up with lightning, and I watched in horror as it struck the side of our boat.

Without thinking, we plunged into the river just as the boat sank beneath the surface. The water was shockingly cold, but adrenaline quickly kicked in as we swam toward the shore.

We knew we had little time. The risk of hypothermia aside, we were certain the fire would attract the guards' attention.

After what seemed like an eternity, we clamoured ashore and lay panting on the sand. Annie was shivering uncontrollably as I held her in my arms.

"We've got to get out of these wet clothes," I said urgently.

But where to go?

34

One of the guards, Larry Broden, saw the flash of fire on the water and rushed to check the interior of the building. He swore as he saw there were no lights on in the facility. Then he discovered the unlocked door. He hurried to Greg's office and saw him slumped over his desk.

He immediately called Derek Avery.

Derek had been going over the latest test results in his Ottawa office, congratulating himself on the progress this group had made. He picked up the phone absent-mindedly and said hello.

"Mr. Avery, there's been a problem at the facility. I found the door unlocked. Mr. Hunt's been knocked out. I saw a fire on the river, and I think maybe someone tried to escape by boat."

"Where's Hunnicutt?" Derek demanded, showing no concern at all for Greg. "Why isn't he calling me?"

Broden explained what had happened earlier with Matthews.

Derek swore. "Listen to me. The control panel's in the wall outside my office. Re-engage the locks and cameras and stay inside the building. I'll be there as soon as I can. And get someone to take Greg to the hospital, for Christ's sake," he added as an afterthought.

****

Hunnicutt was just leaving the hospital when he got the call from Derek.

He was curt. "Get back to the facility right away. Search the rooms. There's been an escape attempt, and I want to know who's missing." He recounted Broden's story of the fire on the water and of finding the facility unlocked and Greg unconscious. "I won't believe whoever escaped is dead until we find the body. Gather your men once you find out who's missing. Take that old bridge on the mainland to the far side of the island and start searching in case he swam ashore."

Hunnicutt didn't think anyone could survive long in those waters, but he knew

Avery was in no mood to be contradicted. "I'll head there now. Matthews is okay. He's got a concussion, and they're keeping him overnight for observation, but he was lucky."

35

I'd struck my ankle on the side of the boat when I dived over, and it was throbbing painfully. We weren't making much headway with Annie having to support me as I hobbled along.

Some instinct of survival made me decide to find an empty cottage. I didn't think we'd present a credible pair in our current condition if we went to one of the lighted houses I could see in the distance.

After ten minutes of awkward walking, Annie pointed to what looked like an abandoned hunting cabin. I nodded to her, and we headed in that direction. When we finally reached the door of the cabin, I started looking around for a rock to break the lock, but Annie simply reached under an old mat on the porch and found the key. She smiled at me. "I guess they don't have too many break-ins in this neck of the woods."

We'd lost our flashlights when we jumped from the boat so I left the door open to allow in what little light there was outside. With the sporadic lightning, the inside of the cabin was lit up, and we managed to find an old flashlight in a kitchen drawer, along with a million mouse turds. Obviously no one had been here for a while, and the mice had claimed the place as their own.

There was an ancient wood stove and some wooden matches, crumpled newspapers, and decaying logs in a metal bin next to it. I had no idea how to start a fire—my mom was never big on the Boy Scouts—but I was saved from the attempt by Annie, who explained that her aunt had a fireplace in her house.

"Let's see if there are any towels and clothes," Annie said and started to search the bedroom of the cabin once the fire was going. There was an old wooden wardrobe in the far corner and she extracted some moth-eaten sweaters and sweatpants.

"These are gigantic, but they'll have to do," she said.

There were no towels in sight anywhere so we grabbed some dishtowels we found in the kitchen. We stripped away our wet clothes quickly, dried ourselves with the small towels as best we could, and then put on the old clothes Annie had found. We dragged the mattress from the bedroom and placed it in front of the fire and sat there warming ourselves until our shivering finally subsided.

Annie laughed suddenly.

"What?"

"I was just thinking that you sure know how to show a girl a good time."

"Well, aside from our boat catching on fire and us almost dying of hypothermia, this part is kind of romantic, don't you think?"

36

Hunnicutt had checked quickly with Broden and found out that Jack Booth and Annie Somers were missing. He and his men had made it across the old wooden bridge that connected the island to the mainland. They were now scouring the island, looking for Jack and Annie.

"Spread out and check the cottages with lights first. Make up a story about searching for a couple whose boat capsized in the river. Look concerned, as if you're here to rescue them."

As luck would have it, the first cottage Hunnicutt came to was the residence of the local caretaker Derek had hired to look after the facility. "Avery already phoned me," he said, as he opened the door for Hunnicutt.

"I've been waiting for them to show up here so I could call you. That is, if they survived, which I severely doubt. I'll let you know right away if I see any sign of them."

Hunnicutt nodded his thanks and went to the next cottage. There were about five or six that had lights on, which surprised him given how early it was in the season.

Guess it's the warm weather. People like to rush spring if they can. The nights must be freezing, though, with the wind off the water. You couldn't pay me enough to live here.

37

Annie and I had unintentionally dozed off by the fire. She shook my arm gently and put her finger to her lips. I listened and then heard what had awoken her. There were muffled shouts in the distance.

I went quietly to a window and saw the beams of flashlights. "Shit! It must be Avery's goons from the asylum. I don't know how the hell we're going to get off this island now that our boat's gone."

"Remember when Greg was taking all of us on the tour of the grounds? He said there was a bridge on the far side of the island," Annie whispered anxiously. "We've got to try to make it to that bridge. We need to leave now and circle behind the guards. How's your ankle feeling?"

Annie had found an old tensor bandage in a cupboard and wrapped it for me earlier. She'd also located a bottle of aspirin that the mice hadn't chewed through. I stood tentatively on my ankle to see how much weight it would bear. "I think it'll be okay. The aspirin helped dull the pain. Let's get out of here."

"I'm going to put the fire out. That may buy us a little time if they don't see the smoke from the chimney." She quietly opened the door of the cabin and returned with a bucket of dirt to throw on the fire. "Okay, let's go!"

We grabbed the flashlight and a dishtowel as a cover to minimize the beam. We were taking a big chance: if they saw the light, that would be the end of us. But we couldn't manage without the flashlight.

Annie and I headed for a copse of trees and directed the beam at the ground, trying to avoid the gnarled roots that seemed to be everywhere. I suddenly realized I had no idea where we were going. "Annie," I whispered urgently, "do you know what direction to go?"

"We came over on the north side of the island. She pointed back to the river. We have to navigate south. Come on!"

I had no idea how she'd determined what direction was south, but I followed her lead, thankful that one of us seemed to know where we were going.

38

Hunnicutt and his men were continuing the search. They'd narrowed it down to the last remaining cottage showing lights in the windows. He knocked on the door, and a white-haired man appeared, looking suspiciously out at him.

"Sorry for intruding on such a night as this, but if I could have a moment of your time. There were some boaters out on the river, and their boat capsized. My men and I are looking for them to make sure they're okay."

The old man looked even more suspicious. "Where'd they come from? Who the hell'd be boating on a godforsaken night like this?"

Hunnicutt tried to remain patient. "They were exploring the ruins of the asylum on the other side."

"Now, that don't make a lick of sense. That place is off-limits. Some rich idiot from Toronto tried to renovate it. I heard he ran out of money, and they closed it down. Why would anyone be there?"

His patience at an end, Hunnicutt demanded: "Have you seen them or not?"

"No, I haven't. And I sure as hell wouldn't tell some mall cop like you if I had. Now get out of here before I call the real police."

He closed the door in Hunnicutt's face.

39

The man waited until the guard had moved on and then called out, "Okay, it's safe to come out now. I don't think that moron'll be back."

Annie and I emerged from the bedroom where we'd been hiding. After stumbling through the woods, we'd seen light in this cottage and decided we'd have to take a chance on someone helping us. The old man had luckily been a good choice for us. He took us in with no questions, let us shower, and gave us some clean clothes. "You two look like the wrath of God," he'd exclaimed.

When we described how Derek's goons were chasing us, his manner had immediately softened. "I don't trust any of them fake cops. The bunch of them're worse than the real ones," he'd scoffed.

I had no idea why he'd be willing to help us until he explained, as he led us into his house, that he was a draft dodger from the Vietnam War. He obviously had his own reasons for distrusting those in positions of authority.

"You can call the police from here, if you want," he said now. "But I wouldn't recommend it. They're apt to take the word of those clowns out there, and not believe you." He chuckled. "Your story's pretty fantastical at that." He nodded toward Annie. "If it weren't for you having that young lady with you, I'd have probably not opened my door."

"Thank you for believing us," Annie said. "I guess we'll just have to wait until they give up and go away, whenever that will be."

"There may be another way," the old man, whose name was Tom, said. "I got a rusty old Jeep in back. Looks like shit but it still runs. I'm willing to lend it to you if you promise to bring it back after this is all over. You'd be taking a chance that they might see you, but I'll draw a map for you with a shortcut to the bridge. Best to go slow and run 'er without lights 'til you hit the bridge. Then gun 'er for all she's worth."

40

We left after thanking Tom profusely and promising to return the Jeep. Annie was driving because she had a better head for directions. I was riding shotgun. We crept along without lights on a road that was barely a path, and I remember thinking that the potholes would probably kill us before the goons got to us. But Annie kept going, managing to keep the old vehicle on the road. I felt a sudden gush of air and realized that the floor beneath my feet was rusted out completely. *Not an ideal getaway car but beggars can't be choosers.*

When we were nearing the bridge, Annie waited, making sure there was no other traffic. Then I lunged back in my seat as she floored it, switching on the headlights as she did so.

The bridge was in almost as bad a shape as the potholed path we'd just left, but at least the goons hadn't counted on us finding a vehicle and hadn't left someone stationed to intercept us.

Now if we could just get over this damn bridge—

41

Greg was finally awake and sitting up in his hospital bed as Derek angrily grilled him.

"I'm sorry, Derek, honestly I am. The storm must have shorted out the system. All I can remember is sitting in my office when the lights went out. I heard some rustling behind me. That's the last thing I remember until I woke up here." He was trying his best to hide the tremor in his voice.

"Well, Hunnicutt hasn't reported in yet so there's still a chance he might find them. You'd better hope so for your sake."

Derek abruptly left the room, leaving Greg to wonder if he'd done the right thing or merely succeeded in putting himself and the others at risk.

42

"What the hell do you mean, you can't find them?" Derek snarled into the phone at Hunnicutt. "They can't have disappeared into thin air. Look again and don't stop until you find them!" He stabbed the off button on his phone.

He took a deep breath and told himself not to panic. He'd minimized the damage as much as he could. Broden was babysitting the other subjects and was grilling them to see if they knew about the escape plot. So far, no one was talking, but Derek was sure they would, sooner or later.

He took stock of his situation. The worst case scenario was that Jack and Annie were still alive and would somehow make it to the police. But he was good friends with a sergeant in the local force. It always paid, he found, to grease palms and cultivate contacts. He called up his phone directory and punched in the number for the police sergeant.

For the first time this evening, he was smiling.

43

Annie and I entered the small police station, silently praying that someone would believe us. We'd agreed on a story that would sound more plausible to skeptical ears.

"We'd like to report a possible crime," I said when the officer at the front desk finally looked up from his paperwork to acknowledge our presence. Hopefully, we looked more presentable now with our change of clothes.

"Sit over there while I call someone to take your statements." He pointed to a waiting area.

We sat on the hard plastic chairs and mentally rehearsed our story. We'd decided to say that we'd been staying with friends in a cottage on the island when we saw lights and heard noises carried across the water from the old asylum. We were concerned that maybe kids had broken into the building because it was supposed to be abandoned. We thought there was a real danger to the kids because we knew, from local accounts, that the building was structurally unsound. It sounded lame as I repeated it in my head, but it was the best we could do. If we actually managed to get a police car out there, it would be up to the rest of our group to convince the cops that they were being held against their will.

The desk officer was fidgeting with his pen and kept glancing furtively over at us. I was beginning to sense something was wrong when Annie nudged me with her foot and nodded toward the door. She had caught the same vibes.

We bolted for the door just as a burly, grey-haired man emerged from the back. "Hey," he yelled at us. We didn't stop but instead climbed quickly into the Jeep, as for the second time that night, Annie gunned it to the floor.

We were about fifteen minutes away from the police station before either of us spoke. She pointed to the fuel gauge that showed empty, and I silently cursed and wondered what else could go wrong for us.

44

Back at the asylum, Eric Chandler had fallen asleep early, but was having a restless night. In his mind, he was once again engaging in an episode of remote viewing. The route around the far reaches of the asylum property seemed vaguely familiar to him. He came across a plot of land with freshly-dug, unmarked graves. This time, the image stayed in his conscious mind when he was awakened by the sound of someone bursting through his bedroom door.

****

Broden had just about had it with this group of weirdos. He'd gathered them all in the dining room of the asylum to question them about the escape of their two friends. So far, all he'd got was a stony silence.

And the way they were looking at him was beginning to creep him out. Hunnicutt had told him they were a bunch of mental freaks, but that was all he knew.

The latecomer to the scene, who had been roused from his bed by another guard, was ushered into the room. "What's your name?" Broden demanded.

"My name is Eric Chandler, and I have something to tell you."

Broden was suddenly all ears.

"There's a cemetery on this property. It has some freshly-dug graves. There are no markers. I can lead you there if you promise not to call Avery or your boss. Otherwise, I'll continue to sit here quietly, and you can dig your own grave by being an accessory to murder after the fact."

****

Broden left the other guard in charge and was now walking behind Eric, watching his every move in case he tried to escape. The beam of Broden's flashlight crisscrossed the ground ahead of him. Suddenly Eric stopped and pointed to a clearing. Broden prodded him ahead. At first, he saw nothing. Then he spotted the six mounds of heaped dirt. The ground had frozen over, so the bodies had probably been buried in the late fall before it froze.

Broden stared for a moment, slack-jawed, at the graves. Then he reached for his cellphone. The reception here was spotty at best, but he finally saw the green bars illuminate on the screen.

He did not call Avery.

He did not call Hunnicutt.

Instead, he dialled 911.

45

We'd found a gas station, and as I was pumping the gas, I pulled a soggy twenty dollar bill from my pocket and handed it to Annie so she could pay inside. She looked as defeated as I felt.

When she returned from paying, I offered to take over the driving and moved the Jeep to the side of the building. I looked over at her. "I'm open to suggestions. Any idea where we should go from here?"

"I checked the telephone book. There was a pay phone outside. I memorized the address for the nearest Ontario Provincial Police detachment. To be honest, I'm not even sure who has jurisdiction—whether it's the local police or the OPP, but I don't know where else we can turn."

"The local police may have already

contacted the OPP. If so, we're dead in the water."

"I guess that's a chance we've got to take."

46

When I pulled into the OPP detachment office, I noticed a reporter with a camera lingering outside. I rolled down my window and waited for a few minutes to see what was up. Two officers emerged shortly, and the reporter immediately confronted them.

"Johnson with the *Kingston Whig-Standard*." The reporter flashed his press credentials at the officers. "Can you confirm the report that graves have been found on the old asylum property, and that there are people being held there against their will?"

"No comment," one of the officers replied brusquely, and the two of them headed for a nearby cruiser, silently cursing the reporter, who had obviously been monitoring police radio frequencies.

I sat in the Jeep trying to make sense of this. "Annie, what graves would they have found? I don't understand." And then a light dawned. "Probably the bodies of the previous group. Remember Greg said he was trying to track them down?"

"But how on earth did the police find out about the bodies?"

"I have no idea, but one of our team must have somehow managed to get word out to the OPP without Derek knowing."

"Jack, that means they'll be rescued. I can't believe it!"

In silent agreement, we left the Jeep and went inside to tell our piece of the story.

****

We sat at the desk of an OPP detective, waiting for him to bring us hot coffee.

He returned with three cups. "It's okay. It's from a machine. I didn't make it so it's safe to drink. Unfortunately, we ate all the Tim Hortons' donuts." He grinned at us, obviously pleased at the chance to poke fun of the cop stereotype.

We smiled back, having gradually relaxed when we realized that he believed our story.

"So you said there was a previous group held against their will and that's who you think the graves belong to."

We both nodded.

"By any chance, do you know if there are family members who could identify the remains?"

"I doubt it. They made a point of choosing subjects with no family ties. The research assistant I told you about, Greg Hunt, will be able to confirm their identities, though," I said.

"Okay, we've sent some officers to the local hospital. Apparently he suffered a concussion."

I grimaced. "That would be my fault. He wanted me to make the escape look authentic."

"It's okay. If you hadn't got out when you did, God knows what would have happened to you."

Annie spoke up. "How did you find the graves?"

The detective consulted his notes. "One of your group—an Eric Chandler—had apparently seen the cemetery. We've sent officers to the asylum to get more information."

Annie and I exchanged looks, realizing that Eric must have stumbled upon the graves while using his power of remote viewing, which frequently became active when he was asleep.

"We owe him a lot. That property is huge. Probably no one would have stumbled upon the graves once the ground thawed and the mounds of dirt had been levelled. There's an old cemetery on that spot. They buried patients there who died in the asylum," he added with an involuntary shudder.

"We owe you two a lot as well," he said. "Your conversation with Greg Hunt gave us the first clue to who was buried there." He hesitated. "You guys look beat. I can send you home in a squad car and then take your full statements in the morning."

"Could you let us return the Jeep we borrowed? Maybe the squad car could follow us and then give us a ride to the asylum. We'd like to thank Eric and see how everyone's doing," I said.

"I'm surprised you'd want to go back there."

"It will be the very last time," Annie said. "By the way, what's happened to Derek Avery? As we told you, he's the one behind all this."

The detective's face hardened. "We're closing in on him," he said simply.

47

It was almost 1 AM, and Derek Avery was moving as quickly as he could through his Ottawa office, shredding documents as he went. He'd left the overhead lights off to avoid detection, and was using a penlight to guide his way.

He would need to relocate: it was probably only a matter of time before details of his past and present experiments emerged. His backers would just have to be patient while he set up shop elsewhere. And what to do about Greg? This was also nagging at his mind. He wasn't completely convinced of the story he'd told regarding the escape. Could he have had a hand in it? Maybe. *Greg and his blasted conscience!*

The sound of footsteps on the stairs caused Derek to pause. He quietly slid open the desk drawer, retrieved the unregistered revolver he'd smuggled in from the U.S., and placed it on his desk. He then heard the sound of a key turning in the lock and realized it must be Greg.

As the door opened and Greg flipped on the overhead light, Derek blinked furiously, his eyes adjusting to the brightness. "What the hell are you doing here, Greg? Your doctor told me they'd be keeping you overnight."

"I signed myself out because I figured you'd be here, Derek. By the way, I've done some research and I know now that you're not *Dr.* Avery nor does any other part of your resume seem to hold water. I should have realized this before. I had enough evidence of your lack of truthfulness. I guess I just didn't want to see it."

Derek snorted. "Well, I guess it's reassuring that you're finally questioning things, Greg, although it's damn inconvenient for me."

"Tell me this much," Greg interjected. "What was the real purpose of the experiment?"

"People like you are so gullible, Greg, that it makes it easy for people like me. There was no higher purpose: no transhumanism, no overcoming human limitations. Pull your head out of your ass for once, Greg, and look around you. There *is* no better world awaiting humanity. If anything, it's *1984* with its doublespeak—or 'alternative facts' as Trump's stooges are fond of calling them.

"The reason why liberal ideology has failed and will continue to do so is that it's drowning in its own morality. There is no more morality, plain and simple. If there was, the Americans wouldn't continue to pollute the planet for the sake of short-term jobs or deprive people of medical care. They wouldn't be streamlining FDA regulations that could potentially lead to a thousand new Thaliomides. But who cares, anyway, as long as the drug company billionaires profit?

"What's emerged south of the border is social Darwinism that ensures only rich white men like the president himself survive. He's a liar, a swindler, and a total hypocrite, but no one gives a shit. They've all drunk the Kool-Aid, and they've been conditioned by the alt-right to regard anyone with a sense of morality as a tinfoil-hat-wearing liberal and an arch-enemy.

"And just look at Europe. It's a tinderbox. A few liberal leaders have survived, but it won't take many more terrorist attacks before the whole continent becomes an armed camp. And then Putin will rush in to snatch up the spoils.

"No, Greg, it's not me who's got it wrong, not by a long shot. It's you."

"That's quite a speech, Derek. So transhumanism is a farce, which leaves what?" He knew now that the whole experiment had somehow been related to the military, but he wanted to hear Derek admit this.

"C'mon, Greg, you're smarter than that. With all the fear-mongering going on, what's the constant that unites the alt-right? Weapons, of course. If you're mentally ill, you probably won't be able to get medical treatment in the U.S., but by God you can still own a weapon, thanks to the NRA lobby. God bless the Second Amendment!

"So my motive, pure and simple, was money. I planned to cultivate and strengthen extra-sensory powers for military use. It's been tried in the past but never to success. And I knew I was the one capable of accomplishing this."

Greg shook his head, almost sadly. "And I actually believed in you. But it doesn't matter now."

"What the hell is that supposed to mean?" Derek demanded. Then he heard heavy footsteps on the stairs and watched as Greg went out onto the landing. Derek could catch snatches of conversation because the door was slightly ajar. He heard the words "search" and "graves," and he understood now why Greg had told him that it didn't matter any more.

He reached for the gun on his desk a few seconds before the door was kicked aside and police officers stormed into the room.

48

One Month Later

All of us were back at university now, and Annie and I had found a small apartment to share. We met up with the others at least once a month just to offer encouragement in the aftermath of our confinement. We were all managing—more or less. Our recovery from the trauma would no doubt be long term.

We heard later that Derek Avery had killed himself rather than face time in prison. From what the police managed to piece together, the head of the security team—I'd since learned that his name was Hunnicutt—had committed the murders under the direction of Avery, who'd panicked when faced with the threat of being charged with unlawful confinement.

Apparently, the other guards had no knowledge of the murders. Hunnicutt had fled, and currently there was a nation-wide warrant issued for his arrest.

Greg Hunt had been co-operative with the police, turning over all his files on the experiment, and we'd explained to the authorities how he'd helped us escape. The police had accepted the fact that he had no knowledge of the murders, but he was still facing charges for unlawful confinement.

At one of these monthly meetings, I got up the nerve to ask the others if they'd heard voices in the asylum walls. I'd talked to Annie about my experience the first night at the asylum, and she told me that she'd sensed the same raw emotions. Jonathan and Adele readily agreed that there were spirits there reaching out to them. Adele said she wondered in retrospect if they were not only trying to convey their own misery, but also to alert us to the danger we were in.

Perhaps now the spirits could find some closure in the fact we'd been rescued and the existence of their graveyard had been reported by the press. I'd heard that some descendants had come forward, hoping to identify the bodies of their family members—their graves marked only by patient numbers—through old asylum records. If they did so, they planned to move the remains to family cemeteries. I dearly hoped this would happen. To be forgotten by history because you were judged unfit to live in society by the standards of the time was a tragedy beyond death.

As for the six of us, we planned to visit the graves of the group who went before us once their bodies had been released by the police for burial. *There but for the grace of God...*

We'd all been changed by our experiences in the asylum, and I'd witnessed how Annie seemed more confident of her talents and less anxious to hide them. She'd switched her major to her first love, English literature, confiding to me that she no longer had to bury herself in the periodic table.

I watched now as she read from a book of Donne's poetry. She twirled the ends of her hair with her finger as she read. It was one of her many small gestures I'd come to love.

She glanced up from her book, saw me watching her, and smiled.

"We're going to be okay, Jack, I think."

"For sure." And for once I did not wait for the sound of the other shoe dropping.

Epilogue

Hunnicutt waited in the darkness outside an abandoned bar in upstate New York. He'd managed to get across the American border without detection.

He heard the sound of approaching footsteps.

A tall, thin man named Palmer appeared out of the gloom. "Do you have them?" he asked Hunnicutt without preamble.

Hunnicutt had found Palmer's name in duplicate files he'd made when he'd burgled Avery's Ottawa office. He'd figured at one point or another, he'd need some form of insurance. He handed the documents to Palmer. "My money?"

Palmer grimaced with distaste as he handed over a brown paper-wrapped package. "I hate this cloak and dagger shit."

Hunnicutt shrugged and started to leave. Then, as an afterthought, he turned back. "Oh, by the way, doc, I guess I should wish you good luck with your experiment. I hope it turns out better for you than it did for your friend Avery."

And with that, he disappeared into the darkness like a ghost.

Acknowledgments

I'd like to thank my husband, Mike McCann, for making the publication of this book a reality. His skills in editing and in cover and book design are greatly appreciated.

I'd also like to thank my readers, Margaret Leroux, Sandra Vanalstyne, Katherine Hooton, and Debra Giles, for reviewing the manuscript and offering suggestions for its improvement.

A special thanks goes to the unnamed gentleman at my "Youngsters of Yore" presentation, who suggested that the asylum outside Ogdensburg, New York, would be a perfect setting for a supernatural novel. I started researching the asylum online and readily agreed that it would make a great setting. I'd previously researched the abandoned Kingston asylum for my novella "Fire Whisperer"so I decided to use details from the Ogdensburg site as well as the Kingston facility known as the Rockwood Asylum for this novella.

The New York site opened in 1890 as the Ogdensburg Asylum for the Insane and was later renamed the St. Lawrence State Hospital. Many of the details of this asylum such as the size of the property and the existence of a nearby island, are taken from historical facts. (Lotus Island was visited by the patients using the steamboat, *Dorothy*, which belonged to the facility.) Other details I have invented for the sake of the story. To learn more about the Ogdensburg asylum, please see http://www.asylumprojects.org/ index. php?title=St._Lawrence_State_Hospital. The site included a cemetery on the property grounds where residents were buried in graves marked only by their patient number. The asylum was closed in the 1980s.

For the Kingston facility, please see http://www. museumofhealthcare.ca/explore/exhibitions/ rockwood-asylum.html.

The idea for this novella originally came from research I'd done on eugenics. I'd been reading historical accounts of Germany in World War II and was struck once again by the enormity of Hitler's slaughter of Jews and other minorities under the guise of creating a master race. I think I'd always assumed that these atrocities had occurred in isolation, but when I started researching the topic of eugenics, I realized I was mistaken. The doctrine of eugenics was espoused in the United Kingdom in the early 20th century, largely as a corollary to Darwinism, and then spread to Canada, the United States, and most European countries. It led to the forced sterilization of mentally disabled persons, prisoners, and minorities; immigration and marriage restrictions; and segregation, as well as in some extreme cases to the practice of euthanasia in hospitals and asylums. (The proposal for the use of gas chambers to perform mass euthanasia in fact came from an American proponent of eugenics.) See https://en.wikipedia.org/wiki/Eugenics_in_the_United_States and https://en.wikipedia.org/wiki/Eugenics. These articles make for chilling reading.

The epicentre of the eugenics movement in the United States was California, which practised compulsory sterilization at a much greater rate than other states. Prior to World War II, American proponents of euthanasia worked enthusiastically with their German counterparts, providing training, conferences, and funding. The Rockefeller Foundation helped found the German eugenics program, and provided funding to the infamous Nazi doctor Josef Mengele up until the time he started working at the Auschwitz concentration camp. See https://historynewsnetwork.org/article/1796.

Transhumanism is an intellectual movement that supports the use of emerging technologies such as nanotechnology; biotechnology; artificial intelligence; and cryonics to advance the condition of the human race in general. See, for example, http://whatistranshumanism.org/. There are many critics of transhumanism, including those who deride it as impractical; others with ethical concerns of man playing God to re-engineer human beings; and many others who fear that it may lead to a resurgence of the practice of eugenics. The two terms are often associated, but the majority of transhumanists do not espouse the latter doctrine. For more information on the subject, please see https://en.wikipedia.org/ wiki/ Transhumanism.

I'd also like to acknowledge my debt to Stephen King's *Firestarter*, which remains one of my favourite of his novels. It's a cautionary tale of governmental abuse of power through the drugging of and experimentation on persons with extrasensory powers for potential military application.

The theme of the unwilling manipulation of the human mind for military purposes has its roots in real-life experiments. For example, MKUltra was the name given to a CIA project that in the 1950s and 1960s made use of subjects, without their consent, for illegal experimentation. The purpose was to identify and develop drugs and procedures for interrogation, psychological torture, and mind control. The project files were largely destroyed after Watergate. However, more than twenty thousand documents have been retrieved under freedom of information legislation, and further documents were declassified in 2001. Many universities, hospitals, clinics, pharmaceutical companies, and prisons willingly cooperated with the project. For more information, please see https://en.wikipedia.org/wiki/Project_MKUltra.

In Canada, Dr. Donald Ewen Cameron was part of Project MKUltra and collaborated with the CIA to conduct LSD experiments on unknowing subjects. Please see https://en.wikipedia.org/ wiki/ Donald_Ewen_Cameron. It's been suggested that Cameron's experiments laid the scientific foundation for the CIA in developing its two-stage psychological torture method. Incidentally, Cameron espoused his own version of eugenics and the elimination of the *weak* in society.

In 1978 the Stargate Project was established under the direction of the U.S. Defense Intelligence Agency at Fort Meade, California. Its objective was to evaluate paranormal abilities, primarily remote viewing, for potential military intelligence-gathering purposes. The project was transferred to the CIA in 1995, and subsequently terminated and declassified after the findings of an independent review concluded there had been no successful outcomes that would warrant its continuation. *The Men Who Stare at Goats* by Jon Ronson is a non-fiction book based on the Stargate Project (which has operated under various other names). The film The *Men Who Stare at Goats* is loosely based on the eponymous book. For further reference, please see https://en.wikipedia.org/wiki/The_Men_Who_Stare_at_Goats.

There are numerous military contractors used by the CIA. Blackwater, now known as Academi, is such a company. It is notorious—hence the name change—for causing civilian casualties in Iraq. Blackwater was founded by Erik Prince, the brother of the U.S. Secretary of Education Betsy DeVos. See https://en.wikipedia.org/wiki/Erik_Prince and https://en.wikipedia.org/wiki/Academi.

The drug Thaliomide, referred to in this story, was created in the 1950s to control nausea and morning sickness in pregnant women. It led world-wide to massive birth defects and infant deaths. FDA regulations for the greater control and testing of drugs by pharmaceutical companies were introduced largely in response to Thaliomide. See https://en.wikipedia.org/ wiki/Thalidomide. At the time of writing, President Trump had eliminated through executive order or refused to sign into law hundreds of regulations, many of which were designed for consumer, wildlife, and environmental protection. He plans to speed up the drug approval process for pharmaceutical companies by eliminating 75 to 80 per cent of FDA regulations. See https://www.raps.org/regulatory-focus%E2%84%A2/news-articles/2017/2/trump-pedges-to-gut-fda-which-regulations-need-to-go.

Finally, in Derek Avery's closing diatribe, he references the "tinfoil-hat-wearing liberal." I borrowed this phrase from an online comment made by a member of the alt-right in response to a mainstream newspaper article critical of President Trump.

About The Author

Lynn Clark was born in New Brunswick and now lives in Ontario with her husband, crime fiction writer Michael J. McCann. She received her B.A. and M.A. in English from Acadia University in Nova Scotia. Prior to her retirement in 2011, she worked for the federal government in Ottawa as an operations manager. She is also the author of *The Home Child*, *Fire Whisperer & Circle of Souls*, and *The Accusers*.

If you enjoyed

THE
PORTAL &
The Experiment

You will also want to read